Havoc!
The Untold Magic of Cora Bell

Havoc!
The Untold Magic of Cora Bell

Rebecca McRitchie
illustrated by Sharon O'Connor

Angus&Robertson
An imprint of HarperCollins*Children'sBooks*

Angus&Robertson
An imprint of HarperCollins*Children'sBooks*, Australia

HarperCollins*Publishers*
Australia • Brazil • Canada • France • Germany • Holland • Hungary
India • Italy • Japan • Mexico • New Zealand • Poland • Spain • Sweden
Switzerland • United Kingdom • United States of America

First published in Australia in 2020
by HarperCollins*Publishers* Australia Pty Limited
ABN 36 009 913 517
harpercollins.com.au

A catalogue record for this book is available
from the National Library of Australia

ISBN: 978 1 4607 5765 9 (paperback)
ISBN: 978 1 4607 1131 6 (ebook)
ISBN: 978 1 4607 8473 0 (audiobook)

Cover design by HarperCollins Design Studio
Cover and internal illustrations by Sharon O'Connor
Typeset in Bembo Std by Kirby Jones
Printed and bound in Australia by McPherson's Printing Group
The papers used by HarperCollins in the manufacture of this book are a
natural, recyclable product made from wood grown in sustainable
plantation forests. The fibre source and manufacturing processes meet
recognised international environmental standards, and carry certification.

For Evelyn Ida. Kick butt. — R.M.

For my fellow travellers,
Glenn, Brad, Chris, Ash,
Robyn and Bill. — S.O.

Chapter One

'**Y**ou're a syphon!' roared King Clang. The fairy king stared at Cora, his blue eyes wide like dinner plates.

Cora Bell squirmed, closing her eye. Her red hair flicked over the scarlet, bumpy scar that covered where her other eye should have been. She was standing inside King Clang's royal hut in The Hollow, the home of the fairies.

Tick and Tock, Cora's fairy friends, fluttered in the air beside her. The fairy brothers were about half Cora's size, with big bellies and lots of hair.

'Father!' whispered Tock to the king.

'Shhh,' said Tick.

The fairy king looked around the hut. 'Syphons are … you … this is …' he spluttered at a much lower volume.

'… bad,' Cora met the king's gaze. 'I know.'

Syphons were magical beings that could absorb

the magic from others. They were considered very dangerous. Cora hadn't always known she was a syphon. In fact she hadn't known anything about magic at all. Cora had been living happily in the port town of Urt with an elderly woman named Dot and her cat Scratch. Cora's world had turned upside down when she accidentally read a spell from a mysterious box that summoned a giant, shadowy creature called a Jinx. Tick and Tock had come to her rescue and they'd fled Urt, not knowing what had happened to Dot and Scratch. With the fairies' help, Cora had battled the Jinx in Jade City, absorbing some of its magic and physical strength. Cora, Tick and Tock had also faced down a warlock named Archibald Drake who had discovered Cora's true identity and from whom Cora had syphoned some warlock magic.

Since the battle in Jade City, Cora had known what she had to do; she had to find others like her. And her family. Tick and Tock had said syphons were hunted and killed for years. She hoped that if there were any of her kind left, they were hidden, safe. Dot and Scratch were also out there, somewhere.

From where he sat on his throne, feet dangling nowhere near to the ground, the fairy king looked warily at Cora. She stood up straight beneath his stare. King Clang's eyes were red and his long beard was bedraggled, sticking up at odd directions like it hadn't been brushed in days. 'I was going to say *unexpected*.'

When they had arrived at The Hollow after leaving Jade City, Fizz, the king's guard, had taken them straight to the royal hut. And it was just as large and as colourful as Cora remembered. Red rugs lined the floor and the roof was decorated with brightly coloured ribbons and flowers. A long table sat to the side, piled high with plates of fruits and berries and nuts. Her stomach gurgled with hunger.

'I have already been summoned by the council,' said King Clang, pointing to a message box that sat on a small round table by his throne seat.

'That was quick,' said Tock.

'They will want to know what happened in Jade City, no doubt,' King Clang said.

'Cora stopped a Jinx from destroying everything,' said Tick proudly.

'She was also the one who brought the Jinx to the city in the first place,' said King Clang sternly.

Tick and Tock grimaced.

'But she stopped a warlock,' said Tock. 'A warlock who was trying to hurt her.'

'And us,' said Tick.

'Which warlock?' the king asked, his small eyes squinting in concern.

'Archibald Drake,' said Cora. The warlock's face entered her mind. His long dark hair, his piercing eyes large with fear as she absorbed his magic. And then his body soaring high over Jade City when the Jinx had thrown him over its shoulder like a doll.

King Clang stopped. 'Archibald Drake?'

Cora nodded. Then, as if in response, she felt the warlock's magic slither beneath her skin. She swallowed.

'Who else knows that you're a ... syphon?' King Clang asked, bending low as he whispered the last word.

Archibald had known that she was a syphon. He had been chasing them for days. What if he was still out there? What if he had survived the Jinx throwing him across the city?

'Just us,' said Tock.

'And Artemis the avian,' added Tick. avians were magical beings that could transform into birds. Cora had met the badly injured Artemis in Jade City. His home in the avian kingdom had been attacked by gremlins and a man with silver hair. Artemis had tried to save the princess of the avian kingdom, but he had been too late. The princess had passed on her powers to Artemis, and in turn Cora had accidentally absorbed the princess's powers from him. Artemis had bravely stood by her side as they faced down the Jinx and Archibald, and she'd promised she would take the tragic story of the princess and the fallen kingdom to the council.

'And where is Artemis the avian now?'

'Home,' said Cora. The first thing they had done when they entered the royal hut was fulfil their promise to Artemis. They had told King Clang all about what happened to the avian kingdom.

King Clang cast his eyes down in thought, his finger tapping the arm of his throne. 'I will tell the council about the man with the silver hair,' he said. 'But they will want to know more about you, Cora.' The fairy king studied her. 'A young girl with one eye defeating a Jinx curse and Archibald Drake. It is … more than unusual.'

Cora nodded.

'You can't tell them she is a syphon,' said Tock.

'No, you mustn't,' said Tick worriedly.

King Clang held up a hand to his sons. 'I know.' He turned his attention to Cora. 'What are you going to do now?' he asked.

Cora didn't need even a moment to think. 'I want to find my syphon family,' she said. Dot's face appeared in her mind. 'And my human family.'

'And we're going with her,' said Tick and Tock at the same time.

Cora swirled around to look at the fairies. 'You are?' she said, surprised.

The fairies nodded, smiling.

And then she didn't know why she was surprised. Tick and Tock had been by her side ever since they'd found her in Urt. Ever since they had saved her from the Jinx.

'You bet your blue boots, we are,' said Tick.

Cora looked down. 'They're brown.'

Before Tick could respond, King Clang flew up from his chair. 'No,' he said, shaking his head.

The fairies whirled on their father.

'What?' replied Tick.

'But Father —' tried Tock.

'It's not safe,' the king said adamantly. 'Especially not for the heirs to the fairy throne and kingdom.'

Tick and Tock rolled their eyes.

'Heirs?' echoed Cora, turning to the fairies.

'We don't know anything about running a kingdom,' said Tick.

'We'll prove it!' said Tock, crossing his arms. 'Ask us anything we should know.'

'What are the three most important things a kingdom must have?' King Clang asked.

'Food,' said Tick.

'Water,' said Tock.

'And ... plumdrops?' tried Tick.

'No,' said the fairy king.

'Jazz music?' tried Tock.

Cora stifled a laugh as she imagined The Hollow full to the brim with plumdrops and jazz music.

King Clang rubbed his temples, exasperated. 'It is still too dangerous. For centuries, syphons have been —'

'Hunted and killed,' said Cora, Tick and Tock at the same time. They had heard it many times before.

King Clang frowned at them. 'It's *more* than that. There are magical beings out there who will do anything —' King Clang stopped himself and shook his head, his small crown tilting from left to right.

Cora thought of Archibald Drake. Is that why he was trying to capture her? Then she noticed something. She couldn't put her finger on it but there was something about the way King Clang looked. Something in his eyes flickered, almost like he'd had this conversation before. He knew something that he wasn't saying and as he avoided her eyes, Cora realised what it was.

'You know where they are,' Cora said softly. 'Other syphons.'

King Clang looked away.

Cora's heart skipped a beat. He did.

'You do?' asked Tock, eyes wide.

'Where are they?' asked Tick.

King Clang sighed. 'It's not safe.'

'You have to tell us, Father,' said Tock.

Cora stepped forward. 'Please,' she said. 'They're my family. They're where I belong. I have to find them.'

King Clang paused as he looked at Cora. 'The council has always heard murmurings. There may have been sightings in recent years. But nothing for certain, only rumours.'

Then, a loud, high-pitched screech ripped through the air outside King Clang's hut.

'What was that?' Cora asked. It sounded like the noise Scratch would make when he was trying to scare off rats in the alleyways of Urt. Only it was much louder.

'Only one thing makes that noise,' King Clang said.

'It can't be,' said Tick. Then he and Tock flew through and out of King Clang's hut. Cora chased after them with King Clang close behind her.

When she got outside, Cora's eye followed Tick's and Tock's to where the screeching noise was coming from. And running down the hill opposite them, in the light of the setting sun, was a swarm of small, green creatures Cora had only seen before in the memory of the princess. The creatures that had helped destroy the ancient avian kingdom.

'Gremlins,' Tock whispered.

And they were heading straight for The Hollow.

Chapter Two

*C*ora watched as the rumbling swarm of small, green, screeching creatures dove down the hillside towards The Hollow. From where she stood, Cora could see row upon row of sharp, pointed teeth glinting in the sunlight. As seconds passed, the screeching only became more piercing. She held her hands to her ears.

'What are they doing here?' Tock asked.

Tick and Tock looked at Cora. *The silver-haired man.* She glanced at the hillside full of descending creatures. The gremlins weren't alone at the avian kingdom. The giant? She paused. The man with the silver hair? Were they here too? She scanned the hillside but couldn't make out anything amongst the close clusters of trees. She felt her magic stir within her.

King Clang whistled sharply and Fizz, along with ten other fairy guards, appeared next to him in *POP!s* of magic.

'Hold them off!' the king ordered over the screeching noise that filled the valley. 'Tick and Tock! Get everyone to safety.'

The fairies nodded.

'And Cora?' asked Tock.

'I'll help hold them off,' she said.

King Clang stared at her in surprise. And then he nodded.

'Be careful,' said Tock to Cora.

'And whatever you do, don't let them spit on you,' Tick said.

'Wait — what?' Cora replied, but Tick and Tock had already disappeared with a *POP!* of magic.

'Into position!' cried King Clang.

The fairy guards formed a line in front of the fairy king, their spears at the ready.

Cora watched the gremlins race towards The Hollow. They were fast. *Incredibly* fast. There was no way, even with the fairies' popping magic that they would be able to get everyone in The Hollow to safety.

Cora took a deep breath and stepped out in front of King Clang and his line of fairy guards. Heart beating fast, she walked out into the space between the guards and the bottom of the hillside. The only thing standing between Cora and the creatures was a cluster of trees.

She could hear snarling and the puffing of breaths as they approached. She grabbed her magic.

Maybe the trees will slow them down?

Then she heard loud crunching sounds like the splintering of wood. Bits and pieces of bark and leaves flew up into the air. Then, a few at a time, the trees in front of her started falling down. The gremlins had torn some of them to pieces.

Nope.

'Hold your position!' roared King Clang.

Then suddenly, the cries in the valley stopped. She could feel the air around her. Hear the rustling of the trees.

Cora stood still, her hands out. She was ready.

Then five gremlins leapt towards her. They dove at her, their claws out, screeching at the top of their lungs. Drool flicked from their mouths and into the air as they ran. And Cora watched as the drool fell to the ground, burning the grass it touched. *That would be the spit Tick was talking about.*

'Now!' cried King Clang.

Using the princess's avian magic, Cora swiftly called up the air around her. It swirled into a whirling gust, faster and faster until it was a roaring wall of air. She sent it barrelling towards the gremlins. It hit them like an invisible wall. They were too small and light to push against it so they were stuck in place, unable to run, unable to move as the wall of wind kept them still.

Cora held her hands up and stepped forward, pushing the wall of wind further against them. The gremlins screamed in anger as they struggled to keep their feet on the ground. Then they were lifted up by the wind and with nothing to hold onto, the gremlins flew backwards in the air, back into what was left of the trees.

Instantly, another group of gremlins dove out to her left. Bright sparks of magic from the fairy guards shot past her towards the gremlins. They scattered back into the trees.

Then suddenly the wall of wind Cora was holding onto fell from her grasp and disappeared into the air like a short, gentle breeze. The princess's magic had stopped.

What? Cora looked down at her hands. 'No, no, no, come on,' she muttered, shaking them. She searched inside herself for her magic. Like ink, it sloshed around everywhere. She reached for the warlock magic. It sparked and sizzled angrily in her grasp.

The gremlins were quick. They took advantage of the still air and sprang through the trees towards her.

All of them. A sea of screeching green, round, red eyes and pointed teeth hurtled towards her into the valley. There must have been over a hundred at least.

Sparks flew at the gremlins from the guards behind her. But this time, the creatures kept running. Some fell to the ground as the sparks hit them. There were so many of them, the fairy magic barely made a difference.

'Hold your position!' cried King Clang.

There were two *POP!s* of magic next to her. Cora whirled around to find Tick and Tock by her side.

'What happened to holding them back?' asked Tick, as he stared at the gremlins bolting towards them.

Cora was about to reply but something inside took hold of her. It was the warlock magic. Looking down at her hands, she saw black sparks flicker from her fingertips. She held the warlock magic and moved her hands upwards, twisting them clockwise in the air, just like she had seen Archibald do in Jade City. The gremlins in front of her slowed and then stopped running altogether.

'That's more like it,' said Tock.

The gremlins stayed still, like they were frozen in place. Then Cora's hands made a quick twisting movement in the air but she hadn't moved them herself. Her hands had moved on their own.

The swarm of gremlins in front of her held on to the sides of their heads with their claws. And then the gremlins grew in size. They grew bigger and bigger, filling with air like balloons. Cora stared at the gremlins in horror. Quickly, she pulled her hands back down to her sides. But the gremlins continued growing bigger and bigger until, suddenly, a splattering crack filled the valley, and all of the one hundred gremlins in front of her exploded! Every single one of them popped into pieces. A wave of green gremlin goo splattered over Cora, Tick and Tock, King Clang and the fairy guards.

Slowly, Cora turned to face Tick and Tock, green goo over her face, her clothes and hands. It was all that remained of the gremlin swarm. Her mouth opened and closed but no words came out. What had just happened?

Tick and Tock stared at Cora, mouths agape and eyes wide.

'Whoa,' whispered Tock.

Chapter Three

The Hollow's fairy guards stepped to the side as Cora, Tick and Tock made their way to King Clang's hut. Still covered in gremlin goo, Cora's clothes made a wet, squelching sound as she walked. Some of the fairy guards shifted their gaze as Cora walked past. Others stared at her curiously.

'What is she?' Cora heard one of the fairy guards whisper.

'She must be a witch,' said one with blonde ringlets.

'Or a demon,' murmured another, hiding his words behind a small, hairy hand.

Cora swallowed. *Demon?* The feeling of so many eyes on her was more uncomfortable than being covered from head to toe in sticky, green gremlin goop.

Tick and Tock, also still covered in what remained of the gremlins, flew next to her.

'That was amazing!' said Tick when they entered the royal hut. 'Cora — 1. Gremlins — 0.'

'You should have seen you!' said Tock.

Cora gave her friends a small smile. She didn't feel amazing. Not even a little bit. She had just exploded a hundred gremlins. She had killed creatures without wanting to, without meaning to. Without needing to. Her hands had moved on their own. She looked down at them, a terrified shiver prickling over her skin.

Inside, the royal hut was empty. Tick and Tock flew over to the table of food and began helping themselves to the berries and nuts. The fairies took turns throwing berries in the air and trying to catch them in their mouths.

'Cora!' Tick called to her, throwing a blueberry in her direction. It bounced off her forehead and dropped to the ground.

'Almost,' said Tock.

Then three loud *POP!s* of magic filled the hut. Cora looked down and was relieved to find herself no longer covered in green goo. And neither were Tick and Tock.

King Clang had entered the royal hut. He flew past them without a word and over to his throne. But he didn't sit down. He flew back and forth in the air, his mind affixed on something.

'And it was gremlins that previously attacked the avian kingdom?' queried King Clang.

'Yes,' said Cora. 'It's the silver-haired man. It has to be. They're working with him.'

Tick and Tock had stopped throwing fruit and flew over.

'The fairy guards searched the forest and found no sign of a silver-haired man or a giant,' said King Clang shaking his head.

Cora paused, confused.

'Gremlins are vicious and uncontrollable creatures. For years they have been kept detained in the Sap Caves by a witch's enchantment,' said King Clang. 'It seems someone has freed them.'

'The silver-haired man,' said Tick.

King Clang nodded.

'Why would they attack The Hollow?' asked Tick.

'A few days ago there were reports of a similar gremlin outbreak west of here, just beyond the Beetle Bridge. They seem to be running wild.' King Clang turned and looked at Cora, his mouth set in a firm line. 'Thank you for … defending The Hollow,' he said. 'Now you must get some rest. The three of you.'

The sun had set over The Hollow but Cora felt like it had been days since she had slept or ate.

Tick and Tock arched their hairy eyebrows at the king.

'It's only five o'clock,' said Tick.

'You need to rest. Especially if you are to head north tomorrow,' said King Clang, looking down at his feet.

'North?' Cora asked. *What was north?*

King Clang sighed.

'There have always been rumours. Small murmurings. Nothing worth the council's time,' King Clang said softly. 'Murmurings that ... syphons were hidden in the northern towns.'

Syphons. Cora's heart leapt. She would have jumped in the air if she wasn't so tired.

Tick and Tock flew up into the air, clapping their hands excitedly.

'You must promise me you will be careful,' said King Clang, pointing at Tick and Tock.

'We're always careful!' said Tick.

'Careful is my middle name!' said Tock.

'I thought it was Lawrence?' replied Tick, confused.

Cora didn't care that they were just rumours or that they were from years ago. It was *something*. And they could start with *something*. She stepped forward. 'Thank you,' she said to King Clang. She wanted to hug him, but she had the feeling he wasn't the hugging type.

The king nodded. 'Look after them.'

Cora watched Tick and Tock twirl happily with one another in the air. She nodded.

'And don't destroy any more cities.'

Cora lay in her hammock. The yellow bedding was strung up from one post to another inside Tick and Tock's hut.

The inside of the fairies' home was messy. Food that looked like it was weeks old lay half-eaten in piles on the grass floor. When she entered, Cora had stepped on a total of three plumdrops after only taking two steps inside the hut, and well-worn socks lay strewn across tabletops, chairs and cups of cold tea. Cora even saw some underwear hanging from a lamp. Tick and Tock's hut reminded her a little bit of the abandoned houses she and Dot would search in Urt. Except it had more food ... and socks.

It didn't take Cora long to pack what she needed for their journey because she didn't have much. Only what she had kept in her pack when she left Urt. Tick and Tock had magicked up a spare set of clothes for her and given her one of their jars of gooseberry honey. They had said it could come in handy if she was ever in a *sticky* situation.

Thankful, Cora added these to her small collection of possessions.

Tick and Tock, on the other hand, had thrown their belongings around, tried clothes on and searched for what to bring with them on their adventure for most of the evening.

'Do I need this?' asked Tick, holding up what looked like a bright yellow flute.

Cora shook her head.

'What about this?' he asked, holding up a tiny, red hat. He placed it on his fairy head. 'It's fashion.'

Cora shook her head at the hat and most of the other things Tick had wanted to take on the journey with him, until at last three small bags lay packed next to one another by the hut's door.

As she lay in her hammock, heavy lumps of guilt and fear squirmed inside Cora. She had *killed* gremlins with her magic. The creatures had died at her hands. She glanced down at her fingertips. Cora didn't recognise them anymore. What was happening to her? And what … what would Dot say if she knew she had … *killed*? Cora lay in silence, thoughts of becoming a monster crowding her mind until the fairies turned to look at her from their matching hammocks strung up nearby.

'Are you alright, Cora?' asked Tock.

Cora nodded, trying to shake the guilt and fear away. But they stayed, lingering like a dense fog.

'I can't wait to see the northern towns,' said Tock.

'Bilg. Berlg. Borlg. Brolg and Broolg,' said Tick peering out from beneath the small red hat. He had refused to take it off.

Cora had no idea where Bilg or Berlg or Borlg or Brolg or Broolg were but she hoped they wouldn't run into any more gremlins.

It wasn't long until Tick's and Tock's loud snores filled the hut. Cora stared into the dark, her mind still cluttered with thoughts. She looked down at her bare wrist. When Dot had found her alone on the streets of Urt five years ago, all Cora had had was an ice-stone bracelet on her wrist. A witch had told Cora the bracelet had been protecting her, protecting her from others, but also from herself. Cora swallowed as she remembered Archibald Drake destroying the bracelet in Jade City. She had wanted to tell Tick and Tock about her bracelet being destroyed but everything since Jade City had happened so fast. She remembered Tick's and Tock's words. *Too much magic and it can … tear you apart.* The magic inside of her did feel … *changed.* Now that she was still, she could feel it slinking around in parts of her.

Cora pulled out Dot's pocket watch from her coat and traced her hand over the cold surface. She hoped Dot and Scratch were alright, wherever they were.

Chapter Four

Cora opened her eye. Worn and cracked buildings sat lopsided and grey in front of her. She could smell the swirling scents of smoke and sea as they tousled the air. Beneath her brown boots lay a rough stone street, broken, bumpy and uneven.

Urt. She was back home. As she gazed out at the drab and withered city, her heart leapt. She had missed it.

Ahead of her, traders lined both sides of the street, selling their wares to the crowd: gold jewellery, hats with ornate feathers, books. Cora watched as one man pulled out an entire chandelier from his top pocket.

Cora politely pushed through the crowd of people in the direction of home. She wondered what Dot was doing. She couldn't wait to tell her everything that had happened since she had left Urt. The Jinx. Tick and Tock. The warlock. The princess. Artemis. Her magical abilities. About being *a syphon*. She hoped Dot would understand why she had had to leave. And she hoped Scratch, her cat, hadn't been too much trouble.

Then a voice entered her ear.

You don't belong here.

Cora whirled around, looking for the owner of the voice. But the crowd moved on either side of her.

Then a shatter of lightning ripped through the sky above her. Cora looked up. The lightning was black. She had never seen anything like it. It spread out like splintered tentacles across the sky, breaking and shattering until it completely covered every inch of the grey Urt sky. Above her a black blanket sizzled and sparked.

You don't belong anywhere, the voice returned to her ear; it was rough like rocks scraping against stone. Cora whirled around once more but this time instead of finding a crowd, she found nobody. The street was empty. Everyone had gone. The traders. The crowd. She was alone in the dark and stormy Urt street.

A loud crack of thunder rippled through the black sky. Cora jumped at the sound. Ahead, she noticed a man standing at the other end of the street, watching her. A man with silver hair. It whipped about behind him dangerously.

'Cora?'

Cora turned around and standing at the other end of the street was Dot. She held Scratch in her arms.

But something wasn't right. She looked different somehow. Then Cora realised what it was. It was Dot's eyes. They were completely black.

You left her here. Alone, the voice returned to her ear.

'But I–I ...' spluttered Cora.

Suddenly, the ground beneath her feet rumbled. The street cracked and shifted, breaking apart in sections. Beneath the street, bright red flames shot up through the cracks.

Cora stepped back and watched wide-eyed as the crack continued down the street, splitting all the way to the ground below Dot's feet.

'Dot!' Cora cried.

She raced towards her, jumping over the cracks, fire rising up from between the cracks and licking her boots.

The street below Dot began to crumble apart.

'Cora!' Dot cried.

Then Cora remembered. She had magic. She held onto the princess's power and tried calling up the air around her. But nothing happened. The magic slipped through her fingers like smoke.

The ground opened beneath Dot. Dot held out a hand to Cora. But Cora was too far away. All she could do was watch in horror as Dot dropped into the fire below.

Cora dove, arms outstretched, she threw her hands into the flames, reaching for Dot. She cried out as the flames burnt the skin on her hands. She held nothing but air. She was too late. Dot and Scratch were gone.

It's just you and me now, said the voice.

Then Cora felt something push her forward, sending her tumbling headfirst into the flickering, red flames below.

Chapter Five

Cora sat up so quickly that she was flung out of the bright yellow hammock and landed face first onto the grass floor below.

'Ow.'

She rubbed her head, her mind a blur of lightning and fire. *Where am I?* Then she heard the soft, tinkling sound of wind chimes and remembered. *Tick and Tock's hut. The Hollow.* She relaxed. It was just a bad dream.

Cora brushed away the food crumbs that stuck to her face from the floor but she couldn't quite brush away the lingering feeling of unease.

'Cora?'

'Why are you smelling the ground?'

She heard the familiar ruffle of fairy wings nearby and looked up to find Tick and Tock fluttering above her, confused expressions on their faces.

'Does it smell nice?' asked Tick.

'It shouldn't,' said Tock. 'We have never, *ever* cleaned.'

Cora sat up straight. 'I wouldn't recommend it,' she said, scrunching up her nose and dusting off more food crumbs from her front. She looked down at her hands. They still felt hot from the flames in the nightmare. *How was that possible?* Then she paused. Running down her right wrist, below her palm, were two, small, squiggly lines. They were black ... like the lightning in her dream.

Cora swallowed.

'What is it?' Tock asked.

'Nothing,' said Cora, pushing her hands out of sight as she stood up.

'We made breakfast,' said Tick, handing her a plate.

Cora noticed that Tick and Tock were dressed in matching aprons. Tall white hats sat on top of their heads and soot dusted their noses.

'Oh, thank you,' said Cora. On the plate sat a pile of irregular-shaped, sloppy, red cakes.

Tick and Tock held plates of their own, stacked high with the same red cakes.

'Berrycakes,' said Tick proudly, shoving one into his mouth.

Cora was picking up a sloppy red cake when a thought occurred to her. 'How are we travelling to the northern towns?' she asked, biting down on the berrycake. It tasted a lot like warm strawberries and only a little bit like grass.

'We will use a gateway to get to Vanir,' said Tock, munching on his own berrycake.

'And then fairy travel to Bilg,' added Tick, licking juice from his fingertips. His plate was already empty.

Cora was about to take another bite out of her berrycake when Tick asked, 'Are you going to finish the rest of those?'

After breakfast, the three of them grabbed their packs and stepped out into The Hollow. Tick and Tock's hut sat on top of a hill that looked out over the wide, blue lake. Cora remembered the first time she had seen the lake. It was right before she had accidentally brought the Jinx to The Hollow. The warm sun glinted off the lake's surface making it shimmer like a jewel.

'Race you!' cried Tick and Tock, and before Cora could answer, the fairies had darted off in the air down the hill, laughter trailing behind them.

'Not fair,' Cora said through puffing breaths when she had caught up to the fairies at the bottom of the hill. 'You both have wings.'

'You should think about syphoning some,' said Tick, spinning in the air. 'They're very useful.'

Cora looked at the fairy's paper-thin wings, imagining herself clumsily flying in the air with a pair of her own.

Tick realised what he had said and stopped spinning. He squinted at Cora and pointed a finger. 'Don't get any ideas.'

Cora laughed. Even though it looked like fun, she wasn't in any hurry to learn how to fly on top of learning how to control her magic. Especially after the dream she'd just had.

Tick, Tock and Cora followed one of the well-trodden paths that led to the centre of the fairy kingdom. Huts of all different shapes and sizes filled the valley. They had rounded, brightly coloured roofs and were made from neatly woven branches, vines and flowers. Cora was happy to see that all the huts had been mended and rebuilt since the Jinx had destroyed them.

Fairies flittered by them as they walked. Some nodded to Tick and Tock, others glanced at Cora and smiled. They made their way to the edge of the valley, following a small path that wove through the village. Soon they came to the large arch at the entrance to the fairy village. Cora remembered it. It sat taller than anything else in the village and was made from many intricately woven branches and flowers.

King Clang wasn't waiting by the arch to see them off. Instead, it was his fairy guard, Fizz, who waited for them.

'Where's Father?' Tock asked.

Cora heard the disappointment in the fairy's voice.

'He left last night to meet with the council,' said Fizz.

Tick nodded. 'Did he say anything?'

'Be careful,' said Fizz.

'Aww, Fizz,' began Tick.

'We didn't know you cared,' finished Tock, trying to give the fairy guard a hug.

'I don't,' said Fizz, swatting Tock away.

Cora gazed out ahead of them into the lush green forest that bordered The Hollow. Deep down in her boots, excitement tickled her toes.

'Are you ready to find your family?' Tick asked.

Cora nodded. *Her family.* It felt strange to hear someone else say it. She couldn't help but think of Dot and Scratch.

Then with a final wave
to Fizz and The Hollow, Cora
and the fairies set off, into the forest,
unsure of what they would find.

Chapter Six

Cora jostled her pack on her shoulders. They had walked until the forest became thick with trees and Cora could no longer hear the lilting wind chimes of The Hollow. The forest stretched on in front of them for what Cora thought looked like days, but she didn't mind. The thought of finding syphons, people like her, kept a small spring in her step.

She ran her hand over the lush green fronds by her side and the rough bark of the wide, twisting oak trees. She felt the small bumps and the sharp, pointed tops. Everything was a beautiful shade of green, the kind that Cora would never have been able to find in Urt. She wished she could take some of it with her, bottle it up somehow, to show Dot. *Green*, she thought with a heavy heart. *Dot's favourite colour.*

Cora felt worry cling to the back of her mind like a bumpy barnacle. Slowly, she pulled her right hand out of her jacket pocket and looked down at her wrist. The two black lines stared back at her, jagged and squiggly. As she stared, Cora thought they looked more and more like … *cracks*. Like in her dream.

'Remember the last time father went to the northern towns?' Tock asked. He and Tick flew about somewhere behind her.

'A woman had turned into a Havoc,' said Tick.

'A what?' Cora questioned.

'Magical beings who have lost control of their powers,' explained Tick.

'Their skin turns dark as night, and their teeth become sharp as knives,' said Tock. He put two fingers near his open mouth like fangs.

'Havocs don't eat. They don't sleep. They don't talk,' said Tick.

'The magic destroys everything in its path,' said Tock.

'And it uses up the magical being, no matter what kind of magic they have, until … until there's nothing left …' added Tick.

Cora's mind whirred. Their skin turns dark? Like the cracks on her wrist? Their magic destroys everything in its path? Like a horde of gremlins? Fear wriggled inside Cora's stomach like a leech. Was she a … a Havoc? With a hand, she slowly reached up and felt one of her teeth.

'Havocs are dangerous,' said Tock.

'Did they fix her? The woman?' Cora asked.

'Nope,' said Tock, shaking his head.

'They were too late,' said Tick.

Cora looked down at her wrist.

'I would never want to be within a fairy arm's length of a Havoc,' said Tick with a shiver. 'That's for sure.'

'Oh, we could never be friends with a Havoc!' said Tock.

Cora swallowed. Perhaps it was best not to tell Tick and Tock about the black cracks. At least, not yet. Not until she was sure what exactly they meant. Maybe there was a way to stop it? She pushed her jacket sleeve over her wrist, covering the marks. 'And,' said Tick, 'when father came back from the northern towns, he smelt of pickled fishtails.'

'Pickled fishtails?' she asked as she stepped over a fallen tree log, relieved for the change in conversation.

'A delicacy in some of the northern towns,' said Tock.

'Though there is nothing *delicate* about pickled fishtails,' said Tick, sticking out his tongue in disgust.

'Why did he go to the northern towns?' Cora asked.

'The council,' said Tock. 'They move around from

one secret meeting place to another secret meeting place.'

'They could meet anywhere,' said Tick. 'Anytime.' He squinted his eyes. '*Secretly.*'

'What do the council do, exactly?' Cora asked.

'They keep order in the magical realm,' said Tock.

'With so many kings and queens, there has to be someone everybody listens to,' said Tick.

'What if you wanted to talk to them?' Cora wondered.

'Not possible,' said Tock, shaking his head.

'They find *you*,' explained Tick. 'And that's never a good thing.'

'It's not?' replied Cora.

'There are six powerful council members,' said Tock. 'Forn Lockwood.'

'Necromancer,' explained Tick.

'Hythia Halfache,' said Tock.

'Witch,' explained Tick.

'Boc Roc,' said Tock.

'Hobgoblin,' explained Tick.

'Plimryll Elm,' said Tock.

'Elf,' explained Tick.

'Sircane Montague,' said Tock.

Tick shuddered. 'Vampire.'

'And father,' said Tock. 'King Clang.'

'Fairy,' explained Tick. 'But you already know that.'

'The magical beings elected to the council change every two hundred years,' said Tick.

Two hundred years?! Was she going to live for that long?' Cora wondered. She tried to picture herself as a two-hundred-year-old woman as she trudged on through the forest.

When most of the morning had passed and the sun peeked through the tree branches and leaves above them, the soft flutter of Tick's and Tock's wings stopped.

Cora, a few steps ahead, turned around to find the fairies standing on the ground, their eyes searching the area for something.

'Have you lost something?' she asked.

'No,' said Tick.

'We're here,' said Tock.

Cora looked around. This part of the forest seemed exactly the same as all the other parts of the forest they had walked through. She couldn't see any sign of a gateway.

Then Tick stepped up to a fallen tree branch that sat on the ground near his feet. He lifted it up, and with it, a round door attached to the forest floor lifted up too. A *hidden* door.

Cora walked over to the fairies and peered down into the dark hole. Stretching down into a dimly lit room was a small ladder.

'Syphons first,' said Tick, standing aside.

Cora stepped onto the ladder and made her way down into the room. When she reached the end, she dropped to the bottom, her boots landing on a wooden floor.

Cora had fallen into a home. Along one of the walls hung shelves overflowing with rows of canned food, and on another wall was a bookshelf heavy with books. She stared at the shelf of books. It reminded her of Dot's. The one they had in their home behind the wall in Urt. Cora noticed that there weren't any lamps. But, somehow, the room glowed as though it were lit by at least two.

In the corner of the room, a lady sat reading in a round, orange chair. She bookmarked the page she was on and peered up at Cora. She smiled.

'Hello,' she said. Her small eyes were framed by a pair of gold-rimmed glasses and her short, white hair had a black streak down its left side.

'Hello,' Cora replied. She felt a little strange dropping down into somebody's living room. She moved her weight from one foot to the other. 'You have a lovely home,' she said.

'Thank you,' said the lady. She glanced at where Cora's eye used to be. 'Need to go somewhere?' she asked.

Cora nodded. 'Vanir,' she said. She hoped she had said the name of it properly.

The woman tilted her head.

Perhaps she hadn't.

Tick and Tock flew down into the room, shutting the hidden forest-floor door behind them with a soft clunk.

The woman raised an eyebrow at the fairies as they flew inside and fluttered next to Cora.

'Hello Ellery,' said Tock with a wave.

'Still reading?' asked Tick.

'You're all going to Vanir?' asked Ellery.

'Father was right; you *are* smart,' said Tick with a smile.

'Remember the last time you went to Vanir?' said Ellery, keeping her grey eyebrow raised.

'It is only for a short time, Ell,' said Tock.

'The fire was an accident,' said Tick.

'And it was not *entirely* our fault,' said Tock.

'Mmm,' said Ellery. 'Tell that to the three centaurs who had their hair completely singed off.'

'We did!' said Tick. 'Numerous times!'

'Doesn't centaur hair grow back?' asked Tock.

Ellery shook her head.

'Oh,' said Tock.

'Whoops,' said Tick.

With a sigh, Ellery reached behind her and pulled out a long stick from behind her chair. At the end of it Cora spotted the same chalk she had seen other guardians use on their travels. And without moving from her seat, Ellery stretched the stick outwards and drew a star shape on the wooden floor in front of them.

The star shape glowed a bright blue before the wooden floor inside it disappeared, leaving a swirl of blue light in its place. The gateway used for travelling throughout the magical world was opened.

Cora thanked Ellery who gave her a nod of farewell. Then she stepped forward and jumped with Tick and Tock into the whirling blue gateway to Vanir.

Chapter Seven

Cora landed on her feet. She paused, surprised. It was the first time she had travelled through a gateway and out the other side without falling or landing in water, in rubbish or on top of a fairy.

'You're getting better,' said Tick.

Cora smiled.

They had appeared in the centre of a town. The wind blew dust about in small tufts where they stood. Cora held her hand up to shield her eye as she peered around. Shop fronts sat either side of them in neat rows and magical creatures strolled past them in the street.

'This way,' said Tick, flying towards the nearest row of shops.

Cora stepped past a round man with a hat so broad it stretched out past his shoulders, and followed the fairies.

She almost bumped into a woman with a pair of pointed tusks that grew down from her mouth, and a lady with scarlet skin who was walking a small, fluffy dog strode past. As Cora looked back at them, the dog's white fur sparkled before changing colour to red.

'What are we doing here again?' she asked the fairies.

'We need a guide,' said Tock as he fluttered ahead.

'Someone who knows the northern towns,' added Tick.

'Do you two not know the northern towns?' Cora asked, a little worried. To be fair, she didn't know the northern towns either.

'The northern towns are vast,' said Tock.

'Vanir is as far north as we have ever come,' said Tick.

'Fairies don't go past it,' said Tock.

'Why?' Cora asked.

'Father always said that the magical beings further north were … *different*,' said Tock.

'Different how?' Cora wondered, hoping it was a good different and not a bad different.

The fairies shrugged.

'If anyone knows the northern towns, it's Gromp,' said Tick.

Gromp?

Cora glanced inside the shop windows to her left. One store sold sparkling gems that grew and shrunk to different sizes, another sold what looked to be wigs made of hair that styled itself. Then Cora saw something in one of the windows that made her stop. It was a poster stuck to the inside of the glass. It had a picture of two incredibly familiar-looking fairies and a large, out-of-control fire. Across the top, words were written: *Fairies and fire don't mix. If you see smoke, it's not a joke.* Then the poster flickered and then showed the fire chasing after two scared fairies.

'Well, that's not ideal,' said Tick, fluttering next to her. 'They didn't get my chin right.'

Cora looked pointedly at her friends.

'We should hurry,' said Tock.

They made their way through the town until they came to a store that sold shoes. Cora looked inside the window at the colourful pairs of boots. And then suddenly Cora jumped back as a pair of blue sandals let out a loud '*LAA LAA LAAA!*'

Tock turned down past the singing shoe shop and Tick and Cora followed.

Against the wall of the shop sat a stack of boxes piled high. Cora continued walking, but Tick and Tock didn't. Turning around, Cora saw that the fairies had stopped at the pile of boxes and were now looking at it intently.

Cora paused, confused.

'It's that one,' said Tock, pointing to a square-shaped box.

'No, it's that one,' said Tick, pointing to a rectangular-shaped box.

Cora walked over to the fairies.

'Gromp,' Tock called. 'It's Tock.'

'And Tick,' added Tick.

Cora spun around. Who were they talking to? There was nobody near them. Well, at least nobody Cora could see.

Tick and Tock waited patiently. And then in front of them, a large rectangular box at the bottom of the pile, opened.

'Told you,' said Tick, sticking his tongue out at his brother.

Tick and Tock flew inside the box.

Cora bent down and peered inside the now-open box. All she could see was darkness.

Then suddenly Tock's head poked through.

'AH!' Cora cried out, falling backwards in fright.

'Come on, Cora,' said Tock, before disappearing inside the box again.

Cora sat up. She looked at the size of the box and the size of herself. She wasn't sure that she was going to fit. Then, bending down, she crawled across the ground and into the open box.

Chapter Eight

It was a tight squeeze. The walls of the box rubbed against Cora's shoulders and arms as she crawled through the dark tunnel. She heard Tick's and Tock's voices coming from somewhere ahead. Just when her knees had begun to hurt, the box tunnel opened up and a large room came into view.

Cora stood up and looked around. A fire crackled from within a hearth to her left. There was a lounge with cushions, and candles sat atop a small round table. A few paintings hung on the walls and there was a kitchen along the opposite wall.

Tick and Tock looked up at her from where they were seated on the lounge. Tick patted the seat next to him, motioning for Cora to sit.

Cora stepped over to the lounge.

'Cora,' said Tick, 'meet Gromp.'

In front of her, by the round table with candles,

was an empty chair. And floating in the chair, by
itself, was a bowl of food.

'Um,' Cora said. She watched the bowl of food
bob up and down in the air on its own and was about
to say hello to it when Tock giggled.

'Gromp,' said Tock, 'meet Cora.'

With a soft crackle, a short man appeared seated
in the chair.

Cora jumped.

'Hello,' said the man. He was small like the fairies,
his feet dangling off the edge of the chair. He had a

messy pile of tangled blond hair on top of his head, and, Cora noticed, a pair of long cat whiskers either side of his round nose.

Gromp held the bowl of food in two hands, and slurped up its contents without cutlery. The food was long like spaghetti. But as Cora looked closer, she could see that each piece of spaghetti wriggled. Like worms.

'Tick and Tock said that you know the northern towns better than anyone,' Cora said.

Gromp smiled at her and nodded, slurping up some worms into his mouth.

'We are going to the northern towns,' said Cora. 'We want to look for,' she paused and glanced at Tick and Tock. The fairies nodded. 'We are looking for … syphons.'

Gromp stopped. A worm wriggled halfway out of his mouth. He quickly slurped it up and placed the bowl down on his lap.

'No,' he said, his eyes firm on Tick and Tock.

'What?' asked Tock.

'Why does everyone keep saying that?' asked Tick.

'You go there all the time,' said Tock.

Gromp shook his head, his whiskers twitching either side of his nose. 'It's different now.' He placed the bowl of worms down on the table. Then with two hands he lifted up one of his yellow pant legs. Stretched across his right leg was a black mark in the shape of a rope, burnt into his skin. It wrapped itself around his leg twice.

'A hunter's trap?' asked Tock, his eyes wide.

Gromp nodded.

Cora remembered what the fairies, King Clang and Artemis had said about syphons being hunted and killed. Then a thought occurred to her.

'Are you a ...' she said.

Gromp shook his head. 'I was collecting tickle fruit in Borlg. When I was halfway up the tree, the tickle fruit shimmered and I realised it was a trap. The fire vines grabbed me. I haven't been back since.'

'Do you have any tickle fruit left?' Tick asked, looking around hopefully.

Tock elbowed his brother.

'What about syphons?' Cora asked. 'Did you see any?'

Gromp shook his head. Cora felt her hopes fall like old leaves from a tree.

Then Gromp paused. 'But there were stories,' he said, 'of a syphon in the northern towns. But there will be hunters,' said Gromp to her. 'There will be traps.'

Cora swallowed. The mark on Gromp's leg looked like it had hurt. A lot. But the possibility that there could be a syphon was all that she needed. She pictured a syphon alone, caught in a trap and surrounded by hunters. Scared. The image tugged at her.

'If it's true,' said Cora. 'If there is a syphon out there somewhere, and there are hunters, we have to help.' She turned to the fairies. 'Don't we?'

Tick and Tock stared at Cora. They nodded.

'Gromp,' said Tick. 'Thank you, but we're going to the northern towns.'

Gromp looked from the fairies to Cora. He sighed. 'It's cold this time of year. Very cold,' he said. Then he hopped down from his chair and walked with a slight limp, over to a cupboard against the wall. He pulled out three coats and threw them to the fairies and Cora.

Cora felt the coat in her hands. It was soft and warm like a furry blanket. But looking at its size, the coat was definitely much too small for her.

'Try it on,' said Gromp motioning to her coat.

Doubtful, Cora put her arms into the coat with difficulty. She didn't get very far when the coat suddenly expanded in her hands as though someone was filling it with air. The coat doubled and then tripled in size, covering her shoulders and stretching all the way down to reach her hands. Cora was swathed in a perfectly fitted coat. It tightened itself around her, moulding to her shape like a warm hug.

When she looked up with a smile, she found Gromp staring at her, a question hidden in his eyes. But whatever it was, he didn't ask it. Instead, he turned to the fairies.

'Should you two be in Vanir?' Gromp asked.

Once their coats were on, Tick and Tock stared at Gromp confused.

'The fire,' explained Gromp.

'That was at least three weeks ago,' said Tick, with a wave of his hand.

'I'm sure everyone has forgotten all about it,' said Tock.

'They haven't,' said Gromp with a smile. Then he moved over to the round table near his chair and pulled open a drawer hidden in the bottom of it. He grabbed something inside the drawer and handed it to Cora.

Cora took it carefully. It was a worn piece of paper that had been folded many times and in many different ways. She opened it carefully. Sketched across the inside were roughly drawn lines and names of places. Lines for paths, rivers, mountains, all intersecting one another. It was a map. There were even small smiley faces and sad faces spread out across it. Cora guessed they weren't supposed to go where the sad faces were.

'Keep to the outer villages,' said Gromp, pointing with his finger to a few of the places on the map.

Cora noticed Bilg, Brolg and Broolg. She nodded. 'Thank you.'

Suddenly, the room filled with a high-pitched sound. It was a voice, singing. '*LAA LAA LAAAAAA!*'

Tick and Tock paused, eyebrows raised. Cora tilted her head. What was that?

Then Gromp shifted his feet and shrugged, glancing down at his shoes. 'They were half price.'

Cora remembered the singing shoe shop they had passed.

'Be careful,' Gromp said to the fairies. He turned to Cora. Again, she thought she saw a question in the man's eyes. But he didn't ask it.

'And if you find any tickle fruit …' said Gromp.

Tick and Tock nodded.

The fairies put their hands on Cora's. She took a deep breath and squared her shoulders, her mind on Gromp's words. And then in a *POP!* of magic, Cora, Tick and Tock, were gone.

Chapter Nine

Cora's boots clunked down onto something beneath her. Like she expected, her stomach sloshed around uneasily. She kept her eye closed until her queasy stomach righted itself. Cora wasn't sure that she would ever get used to fairy travel.

From where she stood, Cora could smell salt in the air and hear the crashing of waves. They were somewhere close to the sea. The cold, salt air reminded her of Urt. Dot had told her once that the smell of the sea was one of the best smells in the world and that sometimes just breathing in the cool air gave her strength. Cora opened her eye.

She stood on a worn wooden boardwalk that jutted out over a dark sea. Unlike the sea in Urt, which was calm and blue, this sea was dark as night. It rolled angrily with waves. With each swell, some of the water splashed onto the boardwalk, wetting the tops of Cora's boots. She looked up to see the sky was dark too. Thunder rolled amongst the heavy clouds above them. It was going to storm.

'This,' said Tick holding his nose closed with two fingers, 'must be Bilg.'

Cora opened up the map Gromp had given her. The word BILG was scrawled near a few wavy blue lines.

'A fishing town,' said Tock, also pinching his nose closed. 'North of mostly everything in the magical world and seemingly twice as smelly.'

The cool sea air washed over her in gusts. Cora breathed it in, letting it fill her with strength. In the distance, she could see the lights of fishing boats bobbing precariously atop the waves. She pulled her furry coat tighter.

'Let's go this way,' said Cora. The fairies turned around and flew down the boardwalk behind her. In front of them, rows of houses and shops sat along the sea's edge, and magical beings scurried in and out of them.

A man in a yellow raincoat stood still by a collection of large wooden barrels. As she approached, Cora noticed that the man had two small horns on his head and two hairy, hooved legs.

Cora looked inside one of the barrels closest to her. Pink lumps sat piled on top of salt. Cora recognised

what the pink lumps were straight away. *Fish guts.*
They sold them in Urt. The next barrel she peered
into was filled with a bright yellow liquid. A sharp,
pungent smell of burning and fish choked the air. She
coughed, certain the stench had singed the insides of
her throat.

'Pickled fishtail?' the man with horns offered. 'It's
a delicacy.'

Cora looked over at Tick and Tock who hid
behind her from the smell, their noses still pinched
closed. They shook their heads vigorously at her from
side to side.

'No, thank you,' said Cora politely.

The man nodded and then placed two round lids
on top of the smelly barrels. 'I would find shelter, if I
were you,' said the horned man. And then he placed
the hood of his raincoat over his head and walked
quickly away, clomping down the boardwalk.

'It's just a little rain,' said Tock, looking up at the
sky.

'Fauns are so dramatic,' said Tick.

They followed the faun down the boardwalk until
they came to a line of stores perched on a walkway
by the shore's edge. Cora noticed that some stores
along the walkway like Tackle Your Fishing Tackle
and another that sold flying boats had signs hanging

over their doors that read *Closed due to storm*. Heavy, shimmering chains also ran down the sides of the stores to large bolts in the ground.

Together, the three of them meandered through the sea town of Bilg.

'Should we spread out?' Tick asked. 'See if there is anything we can find out about the rumours Father spoke about?'

'We must be careful,' said Tock. 'We don't want to attract too much attention. There could be hunters.'

'And we don't want to scare away any syphons,' added Cora.

Tick and Tock nodded.

'Maybe we should try not to mention the word syphon,' said Tock. 'Just in case.'

They spoke to a very kind ghoul who told them about his nephew's birthday party. An elderly gnome who spoke at length about his inner ear troubles. Then they spoke to a not-so-very-kind sprite who told them to leave her alone. They even found a mermaid perched on a rock not far from the shore. Cora waved to her over the gusts of wind, crashing waves and water sprays. But the mermaid had simply tossed her long blonde hair and dove back into the rough sea.

Eventually, nearly everyone in Bilg had retreated to their homes. As Cora, Tick and Tock looked out on the empty town of Bilg, Cora wasn't so sure that their strategy was working. None of the magical creatures they had spoken to in Bilg said anything that seemed at all helpful in their search for syphons.

'Maybe we should try another approach,' Cora suggested.

Loud rolls of thunder boomed above them. They peeked up at the dark, grey sky as a shatter of lightning cracked through it. Then Cora felt a scatter of cold drops hit her skin, one at a time at first, and then all at once until raindrops flew down from the sky in a wave, hitting them like buckets full of iced water. The wind picked up too, blowing in cold sheets from across the sea. Cora held her hands against it.

'I don't think the faun was being dramatic,' cried Cora over the rain and wind.

Tick and Tock struggled to stay in the air, the wind blowing them backwards as they fluttered against it, their tiny wings no match for the gale. Cora held onto the fairies' hands to keep the pair from being blown away as she searched for shelter.

'There,' said Tick, pointing to a ramshackle shed that sat nearby. It was chained to the ground like the other stores and now Cora realised why. She pulled the fairies towards the shed, head down, against the wind. Then, grabbing onto her Jinx magic, she pulled off the lock on the door.

Inside the shed was a collection of fishing rods and nets huddled together. Tock moved the fishing tools aside and Tick made a space for them on the floor.

Cora pulled out Gromp's map of the northern towns. She studied it as best she could in the dim light and listened as the shed rattled and jolted with the wind outside. Cracks of lightning shattered above them.

'Where to next?' Tock asked.

'We could probably walk to Brolg,' Cora said, following a path with a finger that led from one town to the other.

They had only just begun the search for her syphon family but looking down at the map, Cora felt overwhelmed. She had hoped searching for syphons would be like scavenging in Urt; it would take a few days, but no more than a week. Yet the area of the northern towns on Gromp's map was much, much bigger than Urt. It was going to take many, many, many weeks of looking.

Hours passed and the rain, lightning, thunder and wind continued to beat down on the shores of Bilg. The storm outside had settled in. They weren't going anywhere for a while.

Cora lay down on the ground, placing her pack behind her head for a pillow. Tick and Tock did the same but instead of their packs, they used each other as a pillow.

She listened as the rain grew heavier outside. She thought of the syphon Gromp had spoken of. *Please be out there,* she thought.

Chapter Ten

*C*ora ran up a hill, her bare feet padding lightly along the soft grass. She could see Tick and Tock at the top, waving down to her. Nearby, she could hear the wind chimes from the huts in The Hollow. She was almost at the top. Then the sunlight dimmed as clouds above her covered the sky. Looking up, Cora could see that the clouds were black instead of grey. They slunk across the sky like spilled ink.

Shadows passed over the grass in front of her, but Cora kept running until she realised with a painful gasp that her feet were no longer on soft grass. The hill was now a pile of sharp, uneven rocks. Her bare feet scraped against them. But Cora kept running. She ran up the hill until she struggled to catch her breath. Until her feet stung, her legs ached, her lungs burnt. At the top of the hill, Tick and Tock had stopped waving.

Then from behind her, Cora heard a snapping sound and something slimy latched onto her ankle. It pulled her to a stop mid-stride and she flew forward, down onto the rocky ground with a crunching smack.

Cora groaned in pain. She moved a hand up to her face. She pulled her hand back to find blood from a gash near her eyebrow. Cora looked back at her feet. Wrapped around her right ankle was a black, thorny vine. It had shot out of the cracks in the rocky ground and slithered around her leg like a serpent.

Cora tried to kick it off, but it only clung tighter to her ankle. She reached down and grabbed the vine, gasping against the pointed pokes of the thorns, and pulled until the slimy tentacle let go of her. She scrambled up onto her feet and continued up the hill, hobbling this time.

There was another snapping sound from behind her and Cora felt a second slimy vine hook itself around her other ankle, keeping her in place. Before she could turn around and pull it away from her, there was a louder snapping sound and a bigger vine shot out of the ground and wrapped itself around her waist.

'Ah!' Cora cried out as the thorns pierced her body through her clothes. She grabbed onto the vine at her waist and pulled as hard as she could. It broke off and slithered away back into the ground. With her other foot she kicked at the vine on her ankle until it did the same. She raced ahead, up the steep, rocky hill.

Tick and Tock now seemed further away than ever. She waved to them. But they didn't wave back.

Cora heard a snap and turned around to see another vine shoot towards her from the ground. She stepped to the side, moving out of its path quickly. Then another vine curled up from the ground and latched onto her wrist. And then another flew up and grabbed her thigh.

'Tick! Tock!' Cora cried out to the fairies. But they continued to stare back, unmoving.

Cora pulled against the vines and they pulled back, harder. She held still, fighting the black vines with all the strength she had. Her heart dropped as she heard another snap and a long, sharp vine slithered towards her, this time wrapping itself around her chest.

The vines wrenched her down and Cora stumbled, falling to a knee. 'No,' she groaned through gritted teeth. She dug her feet into the rocky ground. Then the vine around her chest tightened.

'Tick! Tock!' she gasped, trying to stand back up. 'Help!'

But the fairies stayed where they were, staring down at her from the top of the hill, as if they didn't know her at all. As if they saw nothing at all.

Cora tried to grab her magic, but there was nothing inside her to grab. Nothing to hold onto. Her magic was gone.

Surrender to us, came the voice that sounded like stone.

Cora ignored the voice. The vines tugged at her harder. She fell down to the rocky ground, fighting against the grip of the black plants that held her. The vines only tightened with every tug, their sharp thorns poking her skin.

Surrender to us, said the voice again.

More black vines shot up and slithered over to her, wrapping themselves around her arms, legs and torso, keeping her still. The vines started to tighten around her.

Cora shook her head from side to side. It was the only thing that wasn't held down by the squirming, black vines. Then as if in response, there was a final snap, and a large vine wrapped itself around her head …

Cora awoke, gasping heavy breaths. She didn't know where she was. It was night-time, rain fell heavily on top of her and in front of her, the sea crashed in waves. What was she doing outside? She should have woken up on the ground, looking up at the roof of the shed they had slept in. Instead, Cora found herself standing up and staring out at the dark and stormy sea of Bilg.

She blinked. *How did I ...?*

Cora stood on the worn boardwalk, her feet balancing dangerously over the edge. She looked down at the wild sea churning below her. Half a step more and she would be *in* the sea. Shakily, she took two steps back, away from the edge.

Rain cascaded down from the sky in sheets, thundering loudly on the wooden boardwalk. Cora wrapped her arms around herself. Her clothes were soaked through. How long had she been out here? She shivered, the cold wind blowing across the rough water, and turned away from the sea. As quickly and carefully as she could, she made her way down the boardwalk. She swiped the rain from her face and her wet hair out of her eyes as she searched for the shed through the rain.

When she found it, Cora opened the door quietly and crept inside, lying down in her spot as though she had never left. Heart thumping, Cora turned over on her side and pushed back her jacket sleeve. The black jagged lines that stretched up from the base of her palm were still there ... but they had doubled in size.

Chapter Eleven

Cora was pretending to be asleep when she heard the familiar rustle and flutter of fairy wings. She had laid awake all night, trying to quell the fear of becoming a Havoc that had seeped into her chest, to settle the uneasy twisting in the pit of her stomach. But the feelings stayed with her, keeping her company, until the morning light crept in through the shed's small dust-covered window.

Tock yawned loudly as he stretched his arms up high over his head and Tick sat up, moving his wings lazily.

Cora waited a moment before sitting up herself. She imagined telling Tick and Tock about the cracks on her arm. About her dreams. But in her mind, she watched them recoil at her monstrous form, their eyes wide in fear ... and then both of them disappearing in *POP!s* of magic ... leaving her alone. *We could never be friends with a Havoc.*

'Not a bad night's sleep,' said Tick.

'Very relaxing,' said Tock.

Cora nodded, but in truth, her whole body ached and her clothes were still damp from the rain. Slowly, Cora stood up. She didn't feel so good. Her magic sloshed uncomfortably within her like one of the boats on the stormy Bilg sea.

'Right,' said Tock, 'no time to dilly.'

'Or dally,' said Tick.

When they left the shelter of the shed, Cora waited for the cool drops of rain to fall. For the wind to prickle her skin with goosebumps. But instead, the sun peeked through a blanket of grey clouds, warming her up.

Following the path on the map, Cora, Tick and Tock trudged through the seaside town. They walked along the shore until they found a dirt road hidden behind a row of boats. Cora noticed some of the boats had wings folded behind them.

As they walked, it was hard for Cora to focus on the direction in which they were heading. Her thoughts were still tangled in her dream. In the marks on her arm. In the way her magic squirmed below her skin.

'I wish we had a little hint as to where the syphons could be,' said Tick.

'Is there anything written on Gromp's map?' Tock asked.

Cora glanced at the map and shook her head. And then a thought occurred to her. 'What is Gromp?' she asked.

'A changeling,' said Tock.

'He can change into anything,' said Tick.

'Anything?' Cora repeated. She tried to imagine the man she met morphing into a piece of fruit.

'Well, most things,' said Tock. 'He can't change into something huge like the sky.'

'Or a lake,' said Tick. 'Or air.'

'And if he changes into another magical being, he doesn't also get their powers. He can only change into the way they look on the outside.'

'And his whiskers?' Cora asked, pointing to her face.

'He changed into a mouse once and has kept them ever since,' said Tock.

'He likes the way they look,' said Tick, with a shrug. 'I wouldn't mind some, myself.' The fairy stroked a pair of pretend whiskers.

'Has he ever changed into you?' Cora asked.

Tock nodded. 'Twice!'

'We played a trick on Father,' said Tick. 'Gromp almost had him fooled but then he sneezed and changed back into himself by accident.'

Tock laughed. 'I will never forget Father's face!'

'I told Gromp not to try it if he had a cold,' said Tick. Then the fairy's eyes went wide. 'Imagine if you syphoned changeling magic,' said Tick.

'Yes,' Cora said distractedly, thinking about her own magic.

'You'd be unstoppable!' added Tick.

'An unstoppable syphon would probably be bad,' said Tock.

'Very bad,' said Tick.

Cora agreed.

'You know what else would be bad?' asked Tock.

'Crooked toenails?' Tick suggested.

'No,' said Tock.

'Frog breath?' Cora suggested.

'No,' said Tock.

'A room full of plumdrops and nobody around to eat them?' Tick tried again, real fear in his eyes.

Tock shook his head. 'If all the food in Brolg was pickled fishtails,' said the fairy.

Tick groaned, sticking out his tongue in disgust.

Cora couldn't help but smile at her fairy friends.

It was past the middle of the day when they saw the next town. Ahead of them, colourful houses balanced at the top of a cliff overlooking the sea. Looking down at the map, Gromp had drawn the town of Brolg as three coloured squares on a hill. And the path they were on wound all the way up to the top.

Below them, over the edge, waves crashed dangerously against the rocks. Cora tried not to think about what would happen if she took another night-time stroll. It was a long, long way down with many, many sharp rocks in between. Cora kept her eyes forward, focused on the brightly coloured town that lay ahead of them.

Brolg.

Chapter Twelve

Instead of a wet, quiet town like Bilg, the town of Brolg was warm and busy. At the foot of the town, a clean cobblestone street stretched out towards a stone fountain. In the centre of the fountain, stood a statue of a merman carved out of a shiny blue stone. He sparkled in the sun, water spouting from each of his hands. Cora watched as the stone merman then moved, bending his arms and legs into a different pose, water this time spouting out of his mouth.

Small cottages and tiny shops sat on either side of the merman fountain. They were painted bright shades of pink, blue and green. In front of her, a round man with blue spots on his skin sat outside a shop playing a musical instrument with all three of his ears. A short, green woman with long, yellow hair that moved on its own handed out pamphlets about the dangers of the rising sea tide. And a man with no legs or arms slithered along the ground. Cora wondered if this is what King Clang had meant about the magical beings being different in the northern towns.

'Look,' said Tock with dismay.

Cora followed the fairy's gaze and noticed a shop to her left that had a sign sitting out the front. PICKLED FISHTAILS. Then she saw the same sign sitting out the front of another shop a little further away. And a similar sign in the window of a shop up ahead, and by the door of another corner store. One sign Cora saw even read FICKLED PISHTAILS. She wondered if they were the same thing.

'What is our new approach?' asked Tock.

Cora wasn't sure. The town of Brolg was much bigger than Bilg. And to be honest, she wasn't even entirely sure what she was looking for. A clue? A feeling? She hoped she would know somehow if she was near other syphons. But all she felt was cold ... and an odd wriggling feeling in her stomach. Her magic.

'You should be able to feel others,' said Tick.

'I should?' replied Cora.

'Did you feel anything when we were in Bilg?' asked Tock.

Cora thought back and shook her head.

'All magical beings have a connection to their kind,' said Tick. 'We probably should have mentioned that earlier.'

'Yes,' said Cora, only slightly annoyed.

'You will know it when you feel it,' said Tock.

'Ours feels like a hiccup,' said Tick.

Cora nodded making sure to pay attention this time to any odd feelings, other than her magic.

The fairies flew off in the direction of a shop called SOUPER and Cora stepped further into the town. She passed a row of magical creatures. They each glided on a pair of tentacles, leaving a trail of bubbles behind them. Cora stepped over them carefully and almost bumped into a woman with one eye. The woman stared at her, surprised. Cora stared back. Unlike Cora's eye, the woman's eye was in the middle of her head. Her skin was tinged purple and she had large, painted red lips. The woman glanced at where Cora's other eye was supposed to be. And then after a moment, the woman nodded and continued on her way.

Cora entered a busy shop to her left that had small cakes with glittering wings flapping up and down inside the shop window. The sweet smells of pastry, fruit and custard filled the shop. Cora breathed them in. The smell reminded her of the time she and Dot had baked an apple. They had traded it for an old pair of wool mittens and it had made their home smell delicious and sweet all day. Scratch had hated it.

Magical creatures waiting to be served stood huddled inside the shop, in front of a long white counter. Numbers were called out and the people in the crowd shot up their hands, which held red tickets. Then cakes and pastries zipped from the counter on glittering wings, over to the customers in the crowd.

Cora's stomach grumbled. The smells swirling around the shop were delicious. Stretching up, Cora stood on her tiptoes, trying to see where she could get a ticket.

As she looked around, Cora spotted a young boy. He stood on the other side of the shop, by the door that customers exited. He was much younger than her, perhaps four or five years old. And he had red hair. It fell down long, past his ears. *Could he be …*

Suddenly, Cora's magic jolted inside of her. It swirled around, filling her up like smoke in a chimney. Was this the feeling the fairies were talking about? Excitedly, Cora pushed through the crowd of hungry customers.

'Excuse me,' she said. 'Sorry. Pardon me.'

A winged pastry hit her shoulder. 'Sorry,' she said to an angry customer. A blue cake slopped custard on her head. Then a chocolate pudding and a croissant flew by her so fast she had to duck out of its way.

When she righted herself,
Cora saw that the boy
was gone.

She moved through
the crowd faster, pushing
past customers and dodging
flying sweets. When she
stumbled out of the door,
half-covered in filling, her
eyes searched for the red-
haired boy amongst the throng
in the crowded town.

Cora found him. She watched as the boy ran up
to a man and a woman, both with matching long, red
hair. He showed them something he held in his hand
and the woman laughed. Then the man picked the boy
up and sat him on his shoulders. The boy laughed as
the man walked around unsteadily. Green tails poked
out below the man's, woman's and child's clothes.

Cora remembered what the fairies had said
about feeling something when she was close to
other syphons. She paused. She felt … nothing. Her
hope fizzled out like a fire in the rain. They weren't
syphons. She stood watching the three of them for a
moment. She couldn't help the feeling of longing that
uncurled itself from somewhere inside her. *A family.*

Then, sharply, something inside of her twisted beneath her skin. She could feel it moving upwards like rising water, searching for a way out. It definitely wasn't the syphon feeling. It was her magic.

Cora breathed deeply. She pushed against the feeling, closing her eye, trying to shove the magic down. When Cora opened her eye again, her vision was blurry. She rubbed her eye but it didn't clear it. She headed for the fountain in the centre of Brolg. When she reached it, she threw her hands on the fountain wall and concentrated on her breathing.

She closed her eye. *In and out; in and out.* She gulped in air. What was happening?

'Are you okay?' came a soft voice from next to her.

Chapter Thirteen

Cora hesitated. Someone was talking to her. Her hands were still clutching the fountain wall. She pushed against the magic that bubbled to the surface and when she felt it subside, she let go of the wall and turned around.

Cora expected to see someone standing next to her but there wasn't anybody there. A man with gills either side of his neck sat on the fountain wall opposite her reading a newspaper. Cora looked at him questioningly. Did he say something to her? When the man noticed her staring at him, he stood up and walked away.

Cora was about to turn back around when she heard the small sound of someone politely clearing their throat. It came from below. Cora looked down.

Standing by her boot was a tiny, winged creature. She was so tiny Cora almost didn't see her. The creature stood peering up at her, curiosity and worry on her tiny face. A pair of paper-thin wings lay still behind her.

What are you? Cora wondered.

'Water nymph,' said the tiny creature.

Cora straightened, eyes wide. *Can water nymphs read minds?*

'No, we can't,' said the water nymph with a giggle.

Cora bent down. The water nymph had sparkling blue skin and bright blue eyes. Even her eyelashes and teeth sparkled. She was beautiful.

Cora held out her hand, and gracefully, the water nymph flittered onto her open palm.

'I'm Merlsa,' said the water nymph. Her voice was high and floated in the air like a song.

'Cora,' she replied.

'You look lost,' said Merlsa.

The water nymph wasn't entirely wrong. Cora felt lost. What if their searching led them nowhere? What if she never found her family? What then? She shook her head free of the thoughts.

'Do you live here?' Cora asked.

Merlsa nodded.

'I'm looking for someone,' said Cora.

'We get all kinds of someones in Brolg,' said the water nymph. 'Good ones ... and bad ones.'

'Bad ones?' Cora echoed.

Merlsa stared at Cora unsure. 'They come at night and head into the woods,' she said. She pointed behind Cora. Below the clifftop town, on the horizon, Cora could see a dark patch of trees.

'Hunters,' Merlsa whispered.

Cora paused. 'Syphon hunters?' she asked softly. Then she remembered that she wasn't supposed to say the word syphon.

But Merlsa nodded.

'What do they look like?' Cora asked.

'Big,' said Merlsa. She stretched out her arms either side of her. 'Mean.'

Then her eyes shifted to look at Cora's eye. 'What's wrong with your eye?' she asked.

'Oh … I, ah, lost it,' said Cora.

The water nymph shook her head. 'Not that one,' she said. She pointed to her other eye. 'That one.'

Cora swallowed. *What was wrong with her eye?*

Then the water nymph grabbed Cora's thumb. 'If you are going to the woods,' she said. The water nymph hesitated. 'Be careful.'

Cora nodded.

And with a smile, Merlsa the water nymph flitted into the air and curtsied. Then she darted away in a sprinkling of water droplets.

Cora paused. *The woods.* That's where they needed to go next. She stood up and searched the crowd for Tick and Tock. Then as a large ogre lumbered past her, something the water nymph had said made Cora stop. She turned and looked down, peering uncertainly at her reflection in the pool of bright blue water of the merman fountain. She stared back at herself and didn't see anything unusual. Slowly, she bent further, looking closer at her reflection. And what she saw made her gasp. She shot up as panic crept over her skin like a slow, wet slug.

Her eye, the only one she had left, was somehow no longer a brilliant shade of emerald green. Instead, it was a dark, swirling ... black.

Chapter Fourteen

*C*ora stared, inches away from the water, and watched in horror as black smoke swirled in her eye like a dark wave. Her eye was like Dot's eyes in her dreams. The dreams with *the voice*. She pulled apart her eyelids with her fingertips for a closer look. *Black*. She blinked rapidly, trying to make it disappear. She looked again. *Black*. Then Cora reached down and grabbed a handful of water from the fountain and splashed it on her eye. She waited and looked down into the pool of water. *Black*. Her stomach churned with unease. What was happening to her?

Cora rubbed her eye roughly with her palm. 'Go away,' she pleaded.

'How rude,' said a voice from behind her.

Cora froze. It was Tick and Tock.

'What are you doing?' asked Tock.

'Are you thirsty?' asked Tick.

Cora waited. She wasn't sure what for. She knew she had to turn around eventually. All she could do was hope that her eye was back to normal.

Slowly, Cora turned to face Tick and Tock. The fairies flittered in the air, curious looks on their faces.

'Yes, I, uh, just needed to wash my face,' Cora said. She held her breath, waiting for the fairies to notice her eye as they studied her face, but as seconds passed, the fairies said nothing.

'We have information,' said Tock, smiling.

With a *POP!* of magic, Tick had his notepad and pen in his hands, and a pair of half-moon glasses across his nose. The fairy flipped through the pages.

'Bloris the dwarf is not happy with the loudness of the fireworks that happen at Brolgfest,' said Tick.

'Fireworks can be very loud,' said Tock.

'Seru the shopkeeper of SWEET SEA TREATS has had to increase his prices across the board.'

'We are not sure exactly which board but one of them,' said Tock.

'Nert the ogre has started a petition for the woods to be moved as lately he has been hearing a ruckus and can't sleep,' said Tick.

'Sleep is important for ogres,' said Tock.

'And fickled pishtails are exactly the same as pickled fishtails,' said Tick, grimacing.

'We accidentally found that one out ourselves,' said Tock.

Cora nodded. The information that the fairies had gathered wasn't exactly what she was hoping for.

'That's all?' Cora asked.

The fairies nodded, proud of themselves.

'What about you?' Tick asked.

'Did you feel anything?' asked Tock. 'See anyone syphon-looking?'

Cora thought of the boy and his family. She shook her head, dismayed. Then she realised what the fairies had said. 'Wait a minute. What did you say about the woods?'

Tick looked down at his notepad. 'Nert is petitioning for them to be moved.'

'It's possible,' said Tock. 'But only with a coven of witches.'

'No, not that,' Cora said her mind whirring. 'Hunters? In the woods?'

Tock nodded.

'A ruckus is a metal human,' said Tick, moving his arms up and down sharply.

Tock shook his head at Tick. 'That's a robot.'

'Oh,' said Tick, continuing to move his arms up and down sharply.

Quickly, Cora pulled out her map. If there were hunters in the woods ... did that also mean there were also syphons? She traced her finger from the word Brolg to an area marked with a cluster of small green triangles. If they left now, they could reach the woods by nightfall. Her heart quickened.

'A water nymph told me that she saw syphon hunters go into the woods,' said Cora. 'Let's go,' she said, stepping away from the fountain. The thought of a syphon being so close was all that filled Cora's mind. In long strides, she walked along the row of shops where a man with a purple beard juggled small, shrieking plants. Suddenly, telling Tick and Tock about her dreams and her eye didn't seem so important.

'Cora, wait,' said Tock. The fairies fluttered after her.

'We should definitely stay away from the woods,' Tick said.

Then Tick and Tock flew in front of her so that she had to stop walking.

'Cora, *you're* a syphon,' Tock whispered.

'I know that,' said Cora.

'So we need to avoid syphon hunters, not chase them into the woods,' said Tick.

'Where there are hunters there could be syphons,' said Cora, stepping around the fairies.

The fairies flew in front of her again.

'Hunters aren't gremlins,' said Tick. 'They're smart.'

'And less slobbery,' added Tock.

'And there will be traps,' said Tick.

Cora remembered the mark on Gromp's leg. She hesitated, and then stepped around the fairies once more.

'Can't we go around the woods instead?' Tick asked.

'Cora, wait,' said Tock.

Cora stopped. 'I saw someone,' she said softly. 'A boy. At first I thought he was ... I thought my magic pulled me to him. He had red hair. He had ... a family, and I ...' she faltered.

Tick and Tock looked at each other.

'If my family is out there ...'

The fairies sighed.

'Fine,' said Tock. 'But at the first sign of hunters we're leaving.'

Cora nodded.

'Pinky stare,' said Tick, holding out his pinky.

Cora grabbed it with hers. 'Pinky stare.'

'Which way are the woods?' asked Tock.

Cora led the fairies out of the town of Brolg and down the road they came up. They headed east along the path, straight for the woods. As the sun dropped lower and lower in the sky, and they got closer and closer to the darkening woods ahead, nerves flittered in Cora's stomach. Was she doing the right thing? Was chasing syphon hunters the answer to finding her family? She pushed against the nerves, and truly hoped that she wasn't leading her friends into danger.

Chapter Fifteen

The faint outline of a wispy white moon peeked down at Cora between the overhanging tree leaves. They had been searching the woods for hours and so far they'd found nothing but an empty chocolate bar wrapper and a pink ribbon that Tick had happily tied in his hair.

The woods weren't like the forest that surrounded The Hollow. The trees were sparse and not bursting with bright, beautiful, lush greenery. There weren't any shrubs or gnarled oak trunks. The trees were narrow and there weren't many places to hide or go unseen. And instead of the sound of birds and soft wind chimes, the woods emitted sounds of croaking insects, and the ominous rustle of wings from somewhere above them.

Cora felt tiredness tug at her eyes and weigh down her feet as her boots crunched atop the dry leaves on the ground. Tick and Tock were so exhausted that they had begun to explore the woods a little *too* thoroughly.

'They're not under this one,' said Tick, putting down a large stone and yawning loudly. He picked up another. 'Or this one.'

'And they're not in this tree,' said Tock, flying down to the ground wearily. 'Or that one.'

All the trees had started to look the same to Cora. She wasn't one hundred per cent sure they weren't going around in circles. The wind had picked up and it blew coldly over the three of them. Cora pulled Gromp's furry coat tighter. She felt her magic roll around. It slithered and stretched uncomfortably beneath her skin.

'If I was a syphon,' began Tick, stroking his chin in thought, 'where would I be?'

'In a bed,' said Tock. He closed his eyes and lay down in the air, his wings fluttering lazily.

Cora turned to her left and something in the distance made her stop. She stared out into the dark woods. Something had moved; she was sure of it. She waited. And then she saw it again, a flicker of light up ahead through the trees. She stepped forward.

'Cora?' came Tick's voice from behind her. 'Where are you going?'

'Is she sleepwalking?' Tick asked Tock.

'She isn't asleep,' said Tock. 'At least, I don't think she is.'

Cora moved past the trees, towards the light. The warlock magic tossed and sizzled, curling away. She tried to ignore it, focusing instead on the light ahead. Was this what Tick and Tock meant? Was this the feeling? Her heart quickened at the thought of what could lie on the other side of the trees in front of her.

'Cora, are you asleep?' Tick asked as he flew worriedly beside her.

'Blink twice if you're asleep,' said Tock.

The fairies waited.

'It's not working,' said Tick. 'She's not blinking.'

'Do you see that?' Cora whispered to the fairies, pointing.

Up ahead, a floating ball of flame came into view. About the size of a dinner plate, the orb of fire hung suspended in the air, like an orange, glowing eye peering at them in the night.

Tick and Tock appeared by her side.

'Wait a minute,' said Tock.

Cora paused as the fairy looked at her.

'What's wrong with your eye?'

There it was. There was no hiding it. Cora was ready to tell the fairies everything. About her bracelet. About her dreams.

Tock flew closer, looking closely at her eye. 'It's black,' said Tock.

Tick joined him, fluttering in the air in front of her. 'Are you sure?' asked Tick. 'It looks more like a very, very dark blue.'

Cora looked away.

Tick and Tock dove in front of her, worried looks on their fairy faces.

'Elephant,' said Tick.

'Explain,' corrected Tock.

'Explain,' repeated Tick.

Tick and Tock crossed their hairy arms over their chests and waited.

Cora didn't know what to say, or where to begin. As she tried to find the right words, something behind Tick and Tock caught her eye.

'Cora?' prompted Tock, waiting.

Cora could only point behind the fairies.

The fairies turned around. Behind them, the small orb of floating fire grew bigger and then split itself into two orbs of fire. And then three, and then four, and more until a long row of fire floated in the air, lighting a path through the forest.

'Oh boy,' said Tick.

Chapter Sixteen

As she stared at the path lit by flames, Cora's heart fluttered with hope. The orbs flickered in a straight line through the forest, lighting the way ahead. 'Isn't this ... couldn't this be ...' she said. *Syphons.*

Tock peered at the ball of flame that floated in front of him.

'It could be,' said Tock.

'Or it could be a hunter's trap,' said Tick.

Cora swallowed. Would hunters really leave a trail of fire through the woods?

Then Tick and Tock looked at each other.

'You go first,' said Tick to Tock, flying behind the fairy and pushing him forward.

'No, you go first,' said Tock to Tick, flying behind the fairy and pushing him forward.

As Tick and Tock tussled, Cora couldn't peel her eye away from the path lit by flames. She felt it pull her in.

'I'll go,' Cora said, stepping forward. What was going to happen once she stepped through? Would it be like the gateway? Would she fall?

Tick and Tock stopped pushing each other forward. They paused, uncertain looks on their faces.

Cora heard a soft hum as she stepped closer.

'Wait!' the fairy said.

Cora stopped.

Tick flew down and picked up a rock from the ground. He threw it down the path ahead and Cora watched as the rock shimmered and disappeared.

Oh.

Bracing herself, Cora took a tentative step forward, moving past the first floating orb of fire. She waited. Nothing happened. She walked forward, past the second orb. Again, nothing happened. When she reached the third floating ball of fire, a strange tingling sensation prickled Cora's skin.

For a second, it felt like being wrapped in one of Dot's knitted blankets — warm and a little scratchy. The humming sound grew louder around her.

'Cora?' came Tock's voice from behind her.

Cora spun around, expecting to see Tick and Tock hovering near, but the only things behind her were more orbs of floating fire in a neat row, stretching through dark forest as far as she could see.

Cora's stomach knotted uneasily.

'Blink twice if you're okay,' Tick's voice called out from nowhere.

Then there was a rustling noise and Cora heard Tock ask, 'How will we see her if she blinks?'

'Oh,' she heard Tick reply. 'Never mind.'

'I'm alright,' Cora called out into the dark forest. 'I think.'

Then suddenly two plump, hairy fairies appeared out of thin air in front of her. Cora cried out as they flew into her, a flurry of wings and arms and legs until all three of them were on the ground in a heap.

'Oops,' said Tock.

'Sorry,' said Tick.

Tick and Tock flew upwards, pulling Cora with them until her feet were firmly on the ground. The fairies hovered in the air, looking up at the trees as they dusted themselves off.

'Witch magic,' Tock said, his mouth in a firm line.

'This way,' Cora said, stepping forward in the direction the flames led.

The three of them made their way through the woods, along the path lit by the fire orbs ahead. In the distance, the trees looked like they went on forever. And as Cora listened, she realised there was something strange about this part of the woods. It was quiet. Not just quiet but … soundless. There weren't any noises at all. From insects to birds. No gentle breeze in the air or soft ruffle of leaves like there was before. Even as her boots trod along the ground, there was no sound of breaking twigs or shuffling soil. It was like this part of the woods was hidden from the rest.

Tick and Tock fluttered in the air next to her, their faces uncertain in the firelight.

'I'm not so sure about this anymore,' said Tick, clasping his hands together nervously.

Every tree and every orb of fire looked exactly the same, repeated in an endless pattern. There wasn't a single leaf or twig out of place.

'That's it,' Tock said, eyes wide. Then Tock stopped in the air beside her. Tick did the same. 'We're not in the woods anymore,' said the fairy in realisation. 'We're —'

But whatever Tock said next, Cora didn't hear it. Suddenly, she couldn't hear anything at all. For a moment, it was like she was under water. Then the humming sound filled her ears once more. And the feeling of a warm, scratchy blanket covered her. She stepped backwards but as she put her foot down, she saw that the ground beneath her was a white marbled stone.

Looking up, Cora saw that the woods in front of her had disappeared and had been replaced with a white, round room. A shallow firepit sat in the middle, throwing light and shadows around her like an eerie puppet show. Behind the firepit stood six stone chairs side by side. In them sat five people she had never seen before. And one she had.

They definitely weren't syphons. Or hunters. So that meant they must be …

The council.

Chapter Seventeen

*C*ora stood still. She glanced briefly to her left and right to find that Tick and Tock were no longer next to her. *Where have they gone?* She looked behind her but only found a stone wall. On the wall, Cora noticed small, intricate symbols carved into the rock. The symbols twisted and turned on one another and reminded her of the symbol that was burnt onto the wooden spellbox she had found in Urt. The one that had held the Jinx curse.

Cora swallowed.

A woman and five men sat still on stone chairs, the glow from the fire flickering ominously across their faces. She glanced at King Clang, who stared back at her evenly.

Then one of the seated men stood up from his stone chair. In the firelight, Cora could see that he was paler than the rest and wore a dark red vest. He had long, white hair that draped down to his shoulders

and he stood tall and narrow. Cora thought
he looked a little bit like a lamppost.

'Hello, Cora,' the man said. His
hollow voice bounced off the stone
walls around them and his small eyes
peered at her interestedly.

*Where am I? And where are
Tick and Tock?* She didn't know
which question to ask first. So
she chose neither.

'I ... I,' Cora
croaked, '... pardon?'

The   man
smiled   down   at
her. It sent a shiver along Cora's skin.

'Do you know who we are?' he
asked.

Cora paused. She tried to remember
the names Tick and Tock had mentioned
at The Hollow when they were telling
her about the members of the council.

'I am Sircane Montague,' said the
pale man. He placed a hand on his chest
and bent down into a long, graceful
bow.

Vampire, Cora remembered.

'This,' said Sircane, turning around and motioning towards a bald man seated next to him, 'is Forn Lockwood.'

Forn had his legs crossed beneath him on his seat and a bored expression on his face. He wore a black cloak and from his neck drooped a silver chain, on which a row of teeth was strung.

Necromancer.

Sircane then motioned to the woman seated next to the necromancer. 'Hythia Halfache.'

Hythia had purple painted lips, a matching purple gown and a nose that looked sharper than a knife. Her unblinking stare rested on where Cora's eye once was.

Witch.

Sircane then turned and motioned to a man whose skin was a light shade of green and his pointed ears poked out of a short tuft of dark hair. He wore a yellow coat with matching pants and his feet dangled far from the ground in his chair. 'Boc Roc,' Sircane said.

Boc Roc nodded at her politely.

Hobgoblin.

'And this,' said Sircane. 'Is Plimryll Elm.' He pointed to the man seated straight-backed in his chair. He had long, golden hair and his eyes were so blue, they almost looked white.

Elf.

Sitting in the chair next to Plimryll was King Clang.

'And of course you know King Clang,' said the vampire. Sircane clasped his hands together and sat back down in his chair.

The six members of the council stared at her. Had she stumbled on their secret meeting? Then Cora remembered what Tick and Tock had said. The council finds *you. And that's never a good thing.* Cora groaned inwardly.

'King Clang told us about the avian kingdom ... and Princess Avette,' the vampire said.

'And the silver-haired man?' Cora asked.

Sircane nodded. 'We are doing all we can to help with the avian kingdom tragedy.' He smiled a smile Cora was sure wasn't a smile at all. As she stared at the vampire's sharp, glistening teeth, a feeling of something not being quite right crept into Cora's gut.

'We would like to know more,' said Plimryll the elf. His lilting voice reminded her of the lullaby Dot used to play. The one that meant *danger, run.*

'More?' she repeated. About the avians? About the silver-haired man?

'How curious,' said Hythia, 'that you, Lora Chime —'

'Cora Bell,' said King Clang.

'Cora Bell,' said the witch, unbothered. 'A little girl from Urt with one eye … could overpower a Jinx curse.'

'And a warlock,' added Forn.

Cora stood still, realisation washing over her like the cold Brolg sea. They didn't want to know more about the avians. Or the silver-haired man. They wanted to know more about *her*. Tick was right. She had walked right into a hunter's trap.

Chapter Eighteen

*C*ora peered at King Clang. How much had the fairy king told them? She glanced around the room, looking for a door or a window or any other kind of way out. Her heart fell when she realised there was nothing.

'We have a few questions,' said Sircane. 'If you don't mind.'

'The warlock,' began Plimryll, 'was Mr Archibald Drake, was it not?'

As if on cue, Cora felt Archibald Drake's dark magic spark inside of her. It swirled up, stretching out like Scratch after he had woken up from a nap.

'Please answer the question,' Plimryll prompted.

Cora had a feeling the elf already knew the answer to his question, but she nodded anyway.

'Where is Archibald Drake now?' asked Sircane Montague.

'I ... I don't know,' said Cora honestly.

The vampire glanced at the others seated next to him.

Cora felt the warlock's dark magic twist beneath the surface of her skin. She needed to find a way out of the stone room. But she couldn't leave without her friends.

'Where are Tick and Tock?' Cora asked.

Hythia Halfache smiled at her. 'They're very worried about you,' said the witch. She held up her hand and pointed a finger at the fire in front of her. Purple sparks flickered in the flames until two shapes could be seen inside the orange blaze. The shapes were Tick and Tock. They were flying around, still in the forest where Cora had left them.

'They're flapping about madly,' Hythia said with a sharp giggle. 'Silly fairies.'

Cora glared at the witch.

'Your eye,' continue Hythia, pointing a short finger at her, 'where is it?'

What? She had no idea *where* her eye was. She just knew it was no longer with her. Why did they want to know that?

'Did a witch take it?' Boc Roc asked.

Hythia turned to the hobgoblin. 'Why is it that whenever there is a limb missing or an organ that's disappeared, it's automatically a witch's fault?'

'What were the ingredients for the last potion you made, Hythia?' Forn the necromancer asked.

'Beetles and pinky toes,' said Hythia, shrugging.

'Answer the question, Cora,' Sircane said.

'I don't know,' Cora said honestly. 'I don't remember.'

'You don't remember losing your eye?' asked Forn.

Cora thought back to the memories she had. The cold rain. The fear. Dot's kind face. She shook her head.

'Overcoming a Jinx curse and defeating a warlock,' said Forn, 'is not possible for a human girl.'

'What do you mean?' Cora asked. She knew what the necromancer meant but she needed time to think. She glanced at King Clang. He remained still, his eyes firm on her. She wanted a small nod or shake of the head. Something, anything, to let her know what to say. Cora knew she couldn't tell them she was a syphon. She couldn't tell them that she had the warlock's magic, the Jinx's magic and Princess Avette's. But she had to tell them something.

'You're not a necromancer,' said Forn Lockwood.

'And you're not an elf,' said Plimryll.

'Or a hobgoblin,' said Boc Roc.

'And you're not a vampire,' said Sircane.

The council stared down at Cora, their eyes quizzical and … impatient.

'So then, the question remains — what are you?' Sircane asked.

Cora paused. She needed a plan. She needed the magic inside of her to stop slithering furiously. Then she realised something. She had something they wanted. Maybe they could give her something that she wanted. *An exchange.* Cora squared her shoulders and met the eyes of the council.

'Bring Tick and Tock here,' Cora said. 'And I will tell you what I am.' She tried to sound confident but she heard her voice shake a little.

Cora's words hung in the air. Sircane sat back in his chair. As Sircane stared at her, Cora stared back. There was something about the vampire's stare. She couldn't tear her eye away from his glimmering gaze. And then before she knew it, she couldn't blink. She couldn't think. Her mind was filled with a fog. It covered everything. What was he doing? For a moment she felt like she could tell him anything. Her biggest fears. Her greatest secrets. Cora felt herself begin to form the words to say she was a syphon. And then the warlock magic jolted inside of her, shaking her out of the daze. She kept her lips firmly closed.

Sircane lifted a finger. And, with a sigh, Hythia clicked her fingers.

Out of thin air, Tick and Tock appeared next
to Cora. They whirled about looking around
them, then when they saw Cora, they flew at
her, grabbing her in a hug.

'We need to leave,' Cora whispered.

'Our magic doesn't work here,' whispered
Tock.

'It's not safe. Wait for my signal,' she
whispered before pulling away from the hug.

'How … sweet,' said Hythia, a look of
revulsion on her face.

The witch clicked
her fingers and Tick
and Tock were
suddenly thrown
headfirst through
the air towards the
firepit.

Chapter Nineteen

Tick's and Tock's faces came to a stop inches from the burning flames.

'Hythia!' cried King Clang, flying up from his seat.

'Stop it!' Cora cried. The warlock magic inside her rolled around. She felt her head begin to throb as she watched her friends squirm pointlessly, trying to get away from the hot flames that licked close to their faces.

'You said you wouldn't harm them!' yelled King Clang.

The witch rolled her eyes.

Sircane threw a clenched fist down onto the arm of his stone chair. The chairs, the floor and even the walls shuddered with the force.

A heavy silence swelled in the room.

The vampire pushed back his ruffled hair.

'Tell us what you are,' said Hythia.

'If you don't,' said the hobgoblin. 'We can't protect you.'

Protect me? So far Cora didn't feel very protected at all. In fact, she felt the opposite.

'Let them go. Let them go and I will tell you,' said Cora, unable to tear her eyes away from her friends.

'Don't, Cora,' cried Tick.

'Quiet!' said Hythia and with a twist of her hand the flames in the firepit roared higher.

'Tell us what you are!' said Sircane angrily. He bared his sharp teeth in a snarl. 'Or we will force it out of you.'

The warlock magic inside of Cora jumped up to the surface. Tick and Tock were in danger. The small amount of control she had on the dark magic inside of her was falling apart like a fraying piece of rope. There was only one thing left she could do. She hoped it would work.

'Okay … I'm a witch,' Cora said softly. 'I'm just a witch.'

Cora let her words sit in the air. They stayed there, floating like feathers. Until a soft cackle blew them away. The laugh echoed around the stone room. And then Hythia sprang up from her seat.

'*Just* a witch?' Hythia echoed as she walked past Tick and Tock. 'There is no such thing as *just* a witch,' Hythia said. 'And every witch knows that.'

Cora could feel her entire body shake from holding the dark magic back. What would happen if she grabbed it? She thought of the gremlins.

Hythia came to a stop in front of Cora. Up close, Cora could see that the witch's skin was a pale grey colour. It glistened darkly in the fire-lit room.

'Do you know why they call it a witch's mark?' asked Hythia pointing to Cora's scar. 'Because some spells require a sacrifice. Spells for manipulation. Spells for location. Spells for protection.' Then the witch placed a hand on top of Cora's head and grabbed a fistful of her hair, jerking Cora's head upwards to look at her.

'You're not a witch,' said Hythia, glancing at her up and down. 'You don't have the bone structure.'

Cora glanced over at Tick and Tock who were still held against the flames. She knew that once she grabbed onto her magic, anything could happen. It also meant showing the council what she was.

'You're right,' Cora whispered. 'I'm not a witch.'

A triumphant smile stretched across Hythia's face.

'I'm ... worse,' Cora finished. She reached a hand upwards and grabbed ahold of the hand Hythia had placed on her head. Using the strength of the Jinx, Cora peeled the witch's fingers out of her hair. Hythia's eyes widened in alarm. Then the witch let

out a shriek as her fingers bent backwards, almost to breaking point.

Plimryll stood up from his seat.

'Leave her, Plim,' said Sircane to the elf. 'We wanted to see for ourselves, remember.'

Tick and Tock. Cora clutched onto Princess Avette's magic. She felt the wind swirl up around her and then she threw it forward towards the firepit. Like extinguishing the wick on a candle, the fire went out and Cora saw Tick and Tock fall safely to the ground before the room was completely eclipsed in darkness.

'What are you —' came a voice in the dark.

'Stop her!'

'Nobody move!'

Cora felt the witch's magic flow through her hand. She heard Hythia gasp and then scream but Cora held on. She heard noises around her but they were drowned out by the thumping beat in her ears as the witch's magic swirled into her. And just as she thought it would, the dark magic came alive under her skin. Cora pulled her hand away from Hythia's quickly. She heard the witch fall to the ground, exhausted.

Then Cora's arm suddenly flew back up into the air on its own and her hand reached out to the magical beings on the chairs. The council. Cora tried to pull her hand back but her arm stayed firm out in front of her. Then she felt herself pull the magic out of another council member's body.

'NO!' Cora cried out. How was it possible? She wasn't even touching anyone! Shouts bounced off the walls and the pounding in Cora's ears grew louder. Cora saw sparks of magic fly back and forth, lighting up the darkness like fireworks in the sky.

She grabbed onto the strength of the Jinx and with her other hand, she pushed against her outstretched arm with all the strength she had until, with a painful thump, it dropped back down to her side.

She felt light-headed as the walls around her slowly spun in the dark.

'Don't let them leave!' came a strangled cry from the other side of the room.

Bright red sparks flew towards her. Cora ducked and covered her head. She stumbled on her feet. Then she heard Tick and Tock fly over to her side, deflecting the sparks that were being sent her way.

Escape. They needed to escape.

Frantically, Cora searched for the witch's magic inside her. But there were so many different things rippling, rolling and sticking to her like oil. She reached for one of them that bubbled like a stew, hoping it was the right magic. Then grabbing onto Tick and Tock, Cora snapped her fingers, just like she had seen Hythia do.

SNAP!

Chapter Twenty

Instantly, the room around them vanished and Cora, Tick and Tock were thrown into a pool of cold water. Cora tried to gasp for air but there was none. There was only water and she was falling down through it like a heavy stone in the deep sea. The coldness stung her skin as it soaked through her clothes. Cora peered through the dark blue but her vision was blurred. She continued to drop deeper and deeper until, suddenly, she felt lighter. Like she was floating instead of sinking. The magic quietened inside her. And Cora sunk slowly down into the deep darkness that waited below.

Cora lay on her bed. She was back home in Urt. Scratch sat next to her, lazily licking his paw. She wondered briefly what it would be like to be a cat. If she were anything like Scratch, it would involve a lot of sleeping.

'What are you doing?' came a voice from nearby.

Cora turned to find Dot, standing by the door. She held her pocket watch in her hand.

'It's time for another drill,' the old lady said. 'Let's go.'

Cora moved to sit up. But she found she couldn't. Something was holding onto her. It was like an invisible hand wouldn't let her move.

'I … I can't,' Cora said through gritted teeth. She pushed against the invisible hand that held her down.

'Don't just lie there,' said Dot.

'No, Dot. I can't move!'

'You're stronger than you think,' Dot said. 'Now more than ever.'

Cora opened her eye. She squinted into the dark blue sea, Dot's words drifting in her mind. She searched inside her for the witch's magic. It was bubbling quietly. Then holding it steady, Cora pushed herself upwards. The magic was like a slingshot, shooting her up through the water like an arrow from a bow. In seconds, she broke the surface.

Gasping, Cora gulped down the cool night air in big, panting breaths. She kicked her legs beneath her to keep afloat and peered around. She was in water. The dark water stretched out either side of her, the light from the stars above reflecting across the water's surface. Ahead Cora spied a beach. But she couldn't see Tick or Tock. Twisting from left to right, she searched for the fairies, but they were nowhere in sight.

Cora took a deep breath and dove back under the water. She pushed herself down and opening her eye, Cora squinted through the deep blue. Below her, drifting downwards, Cora spotted two pairs of wings and four fairy arms and legs.

Tick and Tock were too far down. She couldn't reach them by swimming. Quickly, Cora held the witch's magic that still bubbled close by. She pushed out her palms in the water and pictured Tick and Tock flying towards her. And then, she felt a weight attach itself to her palms, and watched as the fairies shot through the water towards her.

Then before she could run out of air, Cora seized the strength of the Jinx and caught the fairies. Thinking of the shoreline she knew was nearby, Cora snapped her fingers.

In a spray of water, Cora, Tick and Tock landed on the hard ground. Rolling over, Cora coughed and spluttered into the dirt. She turned worriedly, her thoughts on the fairies, and then breathed a sigh of relief when she saw Tick and Tock do the same.

Cora fell on her back, collapsing to the ground in a soaking, worn-out puddle. It felt like she had just been trampled by a Jinx. No, make that three Jinxes. She grabbed her head with a hand and groaned.

'Excuse me, young ladle.'

'Lady.'

Cora opened her eye to find Tick's and Tock's faces only inches from her own. Peering up at them, Cora could see the fairies' faces were red and the little hair that they had on their heads was sticking up at odd angles.

Cora slowly sat up.

'Where are we?' asked Tick. He looked around them. 'And how did we get here?'

Cora glanced around. Behind them stretched a large field of tall grass. The blades looked grey in the moonlight. Each one was so tall that it would've reached up to Cora's shoulders if she were standing up.

'Did you bring us here?' Tick asked Cora.

She nodded. Not sure where exactly *here* was.

'You syphoned the witch's magic,' said Tock.

'We weren't getting out of there any other way,' said Cora. She felt the new magic swirl around inside her. And it wasn't just the witch's magic. She didn't know who exactly the second magic she syphoned belonged to, but it rolled around sluggishly. Cora stared up at Tick and Tock. Everything that she had been keeping from her friends flooded her mind. She had to tell them.

'It wasn't just the witch's magic,' said Cora.

Tick and Tock raised their hairy eyebrows at her.

'I … I need to tell you something,' she said. 'Something happened in Jade City. Something bad.'

Tick and Tock flew closer, worry on their fairy faces.

Cora pulled up her jacket sleeve to reveal her bare wrist. The wrist where her bracelet should have been.

Tick's and Tock's eyes widened.

'Cora, where is your bracelet?' asked Tick.

'It's worse than that,' said Cora. She turned her arms over. Tick and Tock looked down at them. The black, jagged lines sizzled and cracked, moving along her skin. Once no longer than her wrist, they now stretched all the way up to her elbows.

Chapter Twenty-One

The fairies stared at Cora. Tick's mouth opened and closed like a fish. Tock looked like he was about to faint.

Tick grabbed his head in his hands and whirled to look at Tock. 'This is bad.' He flew back and forth in the air, his head still in his hands. 'This is worse than bad,' he said. 'This is a carrot!'

'Catastrophe,' corrected Tock. The fairy grabbed Cora's hand and took a closer look at the lines moving up her arms. 'Cora ...' he said softly.

Tick stopped fluttering back and forth. 'Is this why your eye ...' he said pointing to his own.

Cora nodded. 'I'm sorry I didn't tell you,' she said. 'I should have, I know. But there was never the right time, and ...' she looked down at her arms. They were strange to her now. Like they were somebody else's. 'And I thought, I thought that if you knew, that you would ... leave.' She peered up at the fairies.

Tick and Tock paused.

'We're not going anywhere,' said Tock firmly.

Tick nodded. 'We promise.'

Cora felt like a weight had been lifted off her shoulders. 'But ... I could be dangerous,' she said.

'You can't get rid of us that easily,' said Tock, crossing his arms over his chest.

'People have tried and failed,' said Tick.

Cora smiled at the fairies. It felt good to have them know what was happening to her. For the first time since they set off on their journey, Cora felt her worry lessen.

Tick flew next to Tock and peered at the black lines running up her arm. Then the brothers shared a worried glance.

'Your magic is too much,' said Tock.

'If we don't stop it, you'll become a Havoc,' said Tick.

'But you're not a Havoc *yet*,' said Tock.

'I think my magic speaks to me,' Cora said. 'In dreams,' she explained. 'But like it did with the gremlins, my hand shot up on its own when we were in that room with the council, and I felt it take someone else's magic. I wasn't even touching them.'

'Whose magic?' asked Tick.

'I don't know,' Cora said. It was dark. She really hoped it wasn't the vampire's.

There was silence. A cool wind blew through the tall grass making a soft ruffling sound in the air.

Cora felt a hand on her shoulder. It squeezed gently.

'We will fix this, Cora,' Tick said.

'We will,' Tock added. 'We promise.'

Cora smiled at her friends, relief enveloping her like a warm hug.

'But first, we need to keep moving,' Tock said.

Cora nodded, standing up. She gazed out at the tall blades of grass that sat behind them. She pulled out the map that was in her pack. And as soon as she grabbed it, she realised it was soaking wet. Opening it up carefully, she could see the lines and names Gromp had written were now smudged and unreadable. The sad faces and happy faces drooped sideways. Parts of the map even fell apart in her hands. The water had destroyed it.

'Crud,' she whispered.

'Well,' said Tick, looking over her shoulder at the falling apart map, 'let's hope we're still in the northern towns.'

'And as far away from the council as possible,' said Tock. 'If you took magic from the council, they know what you are. And if they know what you are ...'

'They will be coming for me,' finished Cora.

'And they will be angry,' said Tick. 'Very angry.'

'To the council, the only thing worse than a Havoc,' said Tock, 'is a syphon.'

Chapter Twenty-Two

Cora walked wearily through the tall grass. Her mind was overflowing with thoughts. Thoughts of the council, thoughts of the unusual magic that swam beneath the surface of her skin, thoughts of … *Havocs*. She pictured them as snarling, drooling people with black eyes and black teeth. She tried to shake away the image but it stuck to her mind like a sticky pudding.

They had been walking for half an hour amongst the thick blades of the grassy field. Peering ahead, Cora could see that the grass seemed to stretch on endlessly in front of them. Together, they made a path through the grass by swatting the tall blades out of their way.

'We could be in Mittlelor,' said Tick. 'Father said the grass there was wild like the sea.'

The grass is definitely wild, thought Cora as she swiped at the blades in front of her. One sprung back and hit her in the face.

'Father also said Mittlelor smelt like fruit buns,' said Tock.

Tick sniffed the air and Cora did too. But the air in the field smelt more like old, damp pillowcases than sweet fruit buns.

Tick crinkled his nose. 'Definitely not Mittlelor.'

Wherever they were, the smell hung in the air making it thick and heavy. There wasn't a hint of a breeze. Besides the rustling of the grass with their movements, the field was still. Cora glanced down at her arms for what felt like the hundredth time.

'We could be in the Korkle Plains,' said Tick.

'It's too warm to be the Korkle Plains,' said Tock. 'We must be somewhere else.'

There was silence amongst them as they trudged through the dense grassland. The fear of the council appearing behind her in the tall grass was the only thing that kept Cora moving one foot in front of the other.

'Has anyone ever outrun the council before?' she asked.

Tick and Tock shook their heads.

Cora swallowed, regretting ever asking the question.

'What happened to your bracelet?' asked Tock.

'Archibald melted it in Jade City,' Cora said.

'He melted it?' echoed Tick. 'With fire?'

'No. He just ... dissolved it,' Cora said. 'With his magic. It disintegrated right off my wrist into ... nothing.' Cora remembered watching the bracelet fall from her wrist like snow.

'That's not possible,' said Tock, shaking his head.

'What do you mean? I saw it,' said Cora, pushing blades out of her way.

'The bracelet was tied to you,' said Tick. 'Unbreakable.'

Cora wasn't sure how Archibald had done it, but he had definitely dissolved her bracelet.

'Unless the warlock knows something we don't,' said Tock.

'Well, most magical folk *do* know things we don't,' said Tick.

Tock sent him a sideways glance. 'The members of the council don't know your magic is unstable,' said Tock. 'That's *one* good thing.'

'Amongst a whole lot of very *not* good things,' said Tick with a forced smile.

Cora groaned. Then before she could ask how they were going to stop her from becoming a Havoc, something sharp shot through the grass from behind her. It flew past her, slicing through the air and a blade of grass next to them. Then a whole cluster of

somethings sharp zipped with wild speed through the
air, peppering the blades in front of them with holes.

Tock gasped.

Cora and Tick looked over at the fairy to find him
staring down at his leg. Sticking out of his thigh was a
dart. It was about the length of Cora's hand and had a
small yellow feather tied to the end of it.

'Tock!' said Tick, alarmed.

Tock grabbed his leg and then looked up, his eyes
wide. 'Hunt —,' he said. The fairy dipped in the
air. Tick quickly grabbed onto his
brother, holding him up.

A loud fluttering noise filled the grassy plain with a humming buzz. It sounded like wings.

Cora turned and stood in front of the fairies. Reaching for her magic, she searched through the grass. She saw movement ahead in the bent and broken blades but with only the light from the moon shining down, she couldn't make out much else other than darkness and grass.

Her magic at her fingertips, Cora threw the princess's magic into the grass. Wind soared into the blades, blowing them over and revealing a pair of creatures staring back at them.

There was a woman with yellow hair and hands that glowed red like fire and a short man who knelt on all fours. Then Cora looked up and saw a third soar on wings above them.

'Hunters!' cried Tick. 'Run!'

Chapter Twenty-Three

Cora didn't need to be told twice. She turned on her heel and set off as fast as she could. Tick, carrying Tock, flew ahead of her into the grass. She sprinted after them, brushing the thick blades out of her way, her eyes unmoving from Tick's and Tock's flying bodies zipping in the dark.

Before she could catch up to them, something fell on top of her, bringing her crashing down to the ground. Her face, arms and legs skidded along the dirt. Cora went to get up, to continue running, but as she moved, she realised she couldn't stand. Flipping over to her back, Cora found herself stuck inside a giant net. The ropes that twined together glowed red where they touched her skin. She watched as each strand of rope curled and slithered like a snake.

Grabbing onto the Jinx magic, Cora pushed up against the net. But nothing happened. It didn't budge. The net glowed brighter with her touch. She tried again. Pushing against the ropes. Nothing.

Then the net jolted. It shifted and then lifted up off the ground with Cora inside of it.

Uh-oh.

'Cora!' Tick cried.

She held onto the princess's magic, throwing wind at the net. But the wind bounced right off it, swirling around inside the net. She saw fairy magic hit the net around her. But it was no use. The glowing net deflected every spark as it continued to rise into the air. Quickly, Cora tugged at the swirling magic inside of her again. She held onto the witch's magic and clicked her fingers. She disappeared for a second but then reappeared right back inside the net.

Cora saw the female hunter standing in the grass ahead of her, moving the net with her glowing red hands, a smile on her long face. The male hunter jumped on the spot excitedly as he stared up at Cora inside the net.

'We got one!' he croaked. 'We got one!'

The net moved closer to the hunters. Tick threw magic at the flying hunter who soared above him.

Cora swallowed. She was caught. And she couldn't use her magic inside the net. She stared down at the woman with yellow hair and glowing

red hands. She had a mark on her cheek that looked like the letter S.

Think, she told herself.

Maybe the net was made up of dark magic? She had dark magic. The warlock magic. She felt it now, angry and louder than the rest. She swallowed. She didn't know what would happen if she tried to use the dark magic. But she was moving closer to the hunters in a net she couldn't escape. Below her she saw Tick, still holding Tock, throw magic at the hunters.

The male hunter laughed as he danced around the fairy sparks, before throwing more darts in their direction. Cora watched relieved as Tick dodged them.

It was now or never. Hesitantly, Cora reached for the warlock magic. Black sparks lit up her fingertips. She moved her hand to the sides of the net and touched it. Her fingers curled around the ropes. She focused her thoughts on breaking the net. And like a candle dwindling, the red glow of the net dimmed.

She placed her other hand on the net and the red glow flickered. The whole net wavered in the air. She felt the hunter's magic slowly fade. And then before she knew what was happening, Cora felt herself be pulled from her body.

She was standing on the ground in the grass field. A pair of glowing red hands in front of her. As she saw herself inside the net, she realised she was staring out of a pair of eyes that weren't hers. They were the hunter's.

Tick's fairy sparks of magic flew by her ears.

With a sinking feeling, Cora realised what she had done. *Possession.* She had possessed the female hunter. She stared wide-eyed at herself inside the net.

Then through the eyes of the hunter, Cora watched the glowing net in front of her flicker and suddenly drop from the air, her body inside it falling too. She was a tangle in the now ordinary ropes that plummeted to the ground.

Hurriedly, Cora moved the hunter's glowing red hands up, grabbing her body in the air and gently placing it on the ground.

The male hunter in front of her turned around.

'What are you —'

And quickly, Cora pushed her hands at him, sending him flying through the field of grass.

She had to get back to her own body. *But how?* Cursing the warlock magic, she tried to take control of it and pull herself back into her own body.

Tick continued to send sparks her way. One hit her arm. She gasped as she felt a burning gash rip through her shoulder.

Cora felt for the warlock magic but it was like searching through mud. When she found it, she held on.

Tick shot fairy magic straight towards her just as she felt herself leave the hunter's body.

Cora blinked and found herself lying on the ground, staring up at the night sky. She scrambled to her feet, glad to be back inside her own body. The warlock magic was still in her hands. She tried to shake it from her fingers. And then suddenly, flames ignited the grass in front of her with a *FOOMP!* The flames tore across the field in seconds.

She stared at the flames as they lit up the night, growing larger and hotter by the second, her warlock magic finally slinking back from whence it came. Cora felt dizzy.

The hunter that flew above dove down towards her with a shriek. Cora saw its wings were tattered and torn like a bat's. Her mind foggy, she couldn't think what to do.

Tick appeared with a *POP!* next to her, and then clutching her arm, the fairies and Cora disappeared in a *POP!* from the fiery field of grass as it burnt bright and unstoppable in the night.

Chapter Twenty-Four

They appeared somewhere dark. Cora's stomach lurched with the fairy travel. The air was sharp like ice. And looking down at her feet, Cora saw why. Clumps of ice and snow covered the ground.

'Here,' said Tick.

Cora took Tock from Tick. Peering down at her friend in her arms, she could see that he wasn't looking so good. His eyes fluttered open and closed. The wound in his thigh where the dart pierced his skin had started to bleed.

Tick pulled the bedding from his pack and laid it down. With *POP!s* of magic, a clutter of sticks hit the floor and a small flame swiftly ignited them.

'Where are we?' Cora asked. She fought a chill that crept along her skin. Looking around, Cora realised they were inside a cave made of ice and stone. The opening to the cave was nearby and Cora could see snow splayed out beneath a night sky, falling in drifts.

'The first place I could think of,' said Tick.

Gently, Cora placed Tock on the bedding.

'It looks bad,' said Tick. He wrung his hands together, worry for his brother in his eyes.

In the firelight, Cora could see the skin around the dart in Tock's leg had started to turn yellow.

Then the injured fairy groaned as he opened his eyes. 'Why are we flying?' he asked. 'Are we dragons?' The fairy flapped his arms either side of him.

Cora raised her eyebrow at Tick. 'Dragons?'

Hovering above the dart, Tick peered at it closely. 'Poison,' he whispered.

Poison. Cora hesitated. 'What kind of poison?'

Tick shook his head, unsure.

Cora remembered once after scavenging Scratch had had a small piece of glass lodged in his paw, and Dot had Cora distract the cat while she swiftly plucked it from his paw. Looking down at Tock, Cora thought the fairy seemed distracted enough.

'We need to take it out,' she said.

Carefully, Cora grabbed the dart in one hand. She looked at Tick who nodded at her. Then in one quick motion, Cora pulled the dart from Tock's leg.

Jolted out of his dream, Tock sat upright.

Cora paused, her hand still clutching the dart.

Tick and Cora glanced at each other. They waited for Tock to cry out in pain. But he didn't. He looked at Cora, recognition lighting up his face.

'Hello, Fairy Godmother,' said Tock.

'Hello,' Cora replied.

Then the fairy lay back down, his eyes closing, and soon a soft snore fell from his lips.

'Is there a Fairy Fountain nearby we can take him to?' Cora asked, handing the dart to Tick.

Tick shook his head. 'We're on the edge of the northern towns.'

The fairy held the dart out near the fire for a closer look.

'The poison. Will it ...' Cora couldn't bring herself to ask as she looked down at Tock.

'I don't know,' said Tick, lines of worry creasing his face. He grabbed some snow from the ground and flew over to his brother, placing a small amount on Tock's wound.

Cora watched as Tick gave his brother's hand a gentle squeeze.

'We should take turns keeping an eye on him,' she said. 'I'll go first.'

Tick nodded. The fairy settled down on his bedding.

Cora pulled out her own bedding from her pack and Tock's. 'How did you know about this place?'

she asked. She looked behind her, where the firelight didn't reach and wondered how far the cave stretched behind them.

'I found it,' said Tick. 'Accidentally, when Archibald Drake possessed Belle.'

Cora remembered. Tick had led the warlock far away in the opposite direction, so that she and Tock could escape. Now her friend lay injured in front of her, poisoned with a dart that was meant for her.

'It was snowing then, too,' Tick said. And then, softly, 'Tock loves snow.'

She glanced at the sleeping Tock. She remembered King Clang's words when they left The Hollow. *Look after them.* She hadn't done a very good job of that at all.

It wasn't long until Tick fell asleep.

Huddled in her bedding, Cora watched over the fairies, her mind on thoughts of what had happened in the grass field. Tock was hurt. She had *almost* been captured by syphon hunters. And she had *possessed* another magical being. Something forbidden, even for warlocks. She looked at Tick and Tock. Would they be safer without her? She glanced out of the cave. The snow had begun to fall heavily.

Hours passed and Cora found it harder and harder to fight the pull of sleep. Then a *drip, drip, drip* sound broke into her thoughts. She peered behind her in the

dark. The persistent sound echoed from somewhere further inside the cave.

Grabbing a stick from the fire, Cora stood up and held the light out in front of her, gazing into the dark. Then she took a few steps away from the fairies, lighting up parts of the cave. She walked further into the dark.

The light from the flame she carried bounced off the walls around her until she found the drips from the ceiling of the cave, which fell into a puddle on the cave floor. Right next to the growing puddle, Cora noticed opened cans of food ... and a pack. The pack didn't belong to them. And this wasn't any of their food. Cora stopped.

'Hello?' came a voice at the entrance to the cave.

Chapter Twenty-Five

A boy, carrying sticks and covered in snow, stood at the entrance to the cave.

'Hello,' he said shyly when he saw Cora.

Cora walked over to where the fairies slept, placing herself between them and the stranger. She held her torch up. The boy had light blue skin and short blond hair. He looked older than Cora but not by much. He wore a coat made of fur that fell from his neck down to his feet.

'Is that a hunter dart?' the boy asked, eyeing the dart on the ground near the fire.

Cora nodded. 'But there aren't any hunters here.' She looked at the boy as he relaxed. He didn't seem dangerous. 'I'm Cora,' she said. 'What's your name?'

There was a ruffle behind her. And Tick was suddenly fluttering in the air by her side, glaring at the stranger.

'He's a troll,' Tick whispered. Or at least he *thought* he had whispered.

'Half troll,' said the boy, hearing every word.

'Trolls can't be trusted,' Tick whispered to her again.

'Neither can fairies,' said the boy.

'He could be working for the council,' whispered the fairy.

'I'm not working for anyone,' said the boy.

'He could be a hunter,' whispered Tick.

'I'm not,' said the boy.

'Or worse,' said Tick, giving up on whispering. 'He could be a travelling pickled fishtail salesman.'

'Ew,' said the boy, scrunching up his face.

'A travelling pickled fishtail salesman?' came a voice behind them. Tock groaned as he tried to sit up. He slipped clumsily downwards and Tick flew over to him, helping him up.

Cora knelt down next to the injured fairy.

'How do you feel?' she asked Tock.

'Tired,' he said, a fairy hand on his head. 'Dizzy.' Then he paused. 'Did we see dragons?'

Tick and Cora shook their heads.

'Oh,' said Tock, disappointed. He gazed down at his injured leg and grimaced at the sight.

The blue boy stepped over to them, closer to the fire. He shuffled the sticks in his arms and searched his pockets for something.

'Here,' he said, pulling out what looked like a yellow leaf about the size of his hand. He held it outstretched to Cora and Tick.

Cora paused. What were they supposed to do with a yellow leaf? Eat it? Fan themselves with it?

'For his leg,' the boy said, motioning to Tock.

Oh.

'Rumple Leaf,' said Tick looking over. 'Where did you get it?'

The boy shrugged. 'I like to be prepared.'

Cora looked at Tick. The fairy nodded.

'Thank you,' she said, taking the leaf.

The boy glanced down at her hands as Cora handed the leaf to Tick. She watched as the fairy crumbled the leaf in his hands and sprinkled the pieces onto Tock's wound carefully. The pieces of leaf stuck to the fairy's skin, creating a bandage.

'What is your name?' Cora asked, turning back to the boy.

'Oggmund the Third,' the boy said. 'Pleased to make your acquaintance.' He bent forward in a long bow, a few of the sticks he carried in his arms clonking to the ground.

'I believe it's pleased to make your *accountant*,' said Tick smugly.

'No, it's not,' said Tock.

'Nope,' said Cora.

Tick scratched his head, confused.

'Are they your things over there?' Cora asked, pointing behind her to where she had seen the pack and open food cans before.

Oggmund nodded.

'I think they might be wet now,' Cora said, recalling the dripping sound and puddle of water.

'Oh,' said Oggmund, eyes widening. 'That's not good.'

'You can dry your things by our fire,' she offered. After all, the boy had given them something to help Tock's leg.

Oggmund smiled at her thankfully. He dropped the rest of the sticks in his arms and walked further into the dark cave.

Cora turned to find Tick looking at her sharply, his small fairy arms crossed at his chest.

'Cora, we don't know anything about him,' the fairy whispered. 'He could be anybody.'

'I know,' Cora said.

With his feet, Oggmund pushed all of his things across the ground of the cave to their fire. He sat down with a thump and put his hands out, warming them up near the flames. He smiled at them.

Tick's arms were still crossed as he glared at the stranger across the flames. 'It's my turn to keep watch.'

Cora wasn't sure about leaving Tick alone with Oggmund but she was struggling to keep her eyes open.

She nodded thankfully at the fairy and lay down next to Tock in her bedding. It wasn't long until the crackling of the fire was the last thing she heard before falling asleep.

Chapter Twenty-Six

Cora stood up. Tall, thin trees stretched up beside her. Peering around, she recognised her surroundings as the woods near Brolg. But what was she doing here? And where were Tick and Tock?

'Tick,' she called into the forest. 'Tock.'

Cora took a few steps forward and stopped when she saw the air in front of her shimmer. But it wasn't Tick or Tock who appeared. It was a man with long, dark hair and a familiar pair of piercing eyes. It was someone she had hoped she would never see again. Archibald Drake.

The warlock stared down at her.

'My, my,' he said. 'Look what you've become.'

Cora looked down.

Black cracks covered her entire body. They wound their way up from her toes, covering every inch of her.

The warlock moved his hands and a silver liquid appeared, swirling in the air in front of her.

Cora stared at her reflection and what she saw frightened her. The girl who stared back wasn't her anymore. Her skin was grey. The black cracks stretched up all the way to her neck. She reached up with a crumbling hand and touched her cheek. It was cold. Her eye, black and sunken, looked hollow. She was an echo of her former self.

A Havoc.

'I told you you're not strong enough,' the warlock said.

'Without that bracelet, the dark magic is eating you alive.'

Angrily, Cora pushed the silver liquid away from her with her hand and it flew towards the warlock. It went through him, disappearing in the air.

The warlock smiled at her.

Then from the darkness, shapes stepped into view. One after another, the vampire, the witch, the necromancer, the hobgoblin, the elf and King Clang came forward. Each member of the council stared at her, eyes accusing.

'It won't be long until they find you,' said the warlock.

The witch laughed. The high-pitched sound bounced around the woods.

'But,' said Cora. 'King Clang,' she tried.

'An out-of-control syphon,' said King Clang, shaking his head. 'There's no greater risk to the magical world.'

Then two *POP!s* of magic filled the air and Tick and Tock appeared, flying by their father's side. They stared at Cora like they didn't know her.

A crack of lightning shot through the woods ahead, and the silver-haired man stood in the distance, his hair sharp like knives.

'Don't bother fighting it,' said the warlock, stepping forward. 'You're almost ours.' Archibald smiled at her, his teeth pointed. The silver-haired man and the council did the same, their faces stretching into sinister smiles as they strode towards her.

Cora stepped back until she felt something large behind her. Spinning around, she looked up to find an enormous shadow creature, its yellow eyes like beacons in the night. *The Jinx.* But instead of staring at her, it stared at Archibald, the council and the man with silver hair.

Next to the Jinx stood a young girl in a yellow nightdress. Cora had only seen her in Artemis's memories. But she knew who she was. *Princess Avette.* The young girl nodded at Cora, squaring her shoulders at the group of people behind her.

The Jinx roared loudly at them.

Cora realised … she wasn't alone.

Turning around, Cora's magic sparked at her fingertips. Archibald Drake's stare faltered.

Cora watched as the council stepped back into the darkness with Tick and Tock. And then in a crack of lightning, the man with silver hair did the same. Until only Archibald Drake was left standing in the woods. Finally, the warlock shimmered, disappearing into the night, a low laugh on his lips.

Chapter Twenty-Seven

When Cora woke, she was relieved to see that she was no longer in the woods, but the cave they had camped in overnight. Her bones clicked as she stretched upwards, blinking at the sunlight that peeked through the cave. It was morning.

Opposite her, Oggmund lay asleep on his bedding. She looked over at Tick who was meant to be keeping watch. But the fairy was fast asleep. And so was Tock.

Glancing down at the fairy's leg, she could see the wound was almost healed.

Cora sat up and waited for the sun's soft rays to warm her. But as she moved, something didn't feel right. Her head spun. She was cold. She grabbed some sticks and put them on the fire that burnt low.

Her thoughts were on her dream.

She moved closer to the fire as the flames took hold of the kindling sticks.

Maybe she was hungry. When was the last time they had eaten?

The troll stirred awake. He let out a long yawn before sitting up.

'Do you usually talk in your sleep?' Oggmund asked.

Cora stopped. *Uh-oh.*

'Wh-what did I say?' she asked, trying not to show the panic that she felt. Had she revealed she was a syphon?

Oggmund shrugged. 'It wasn't clear.'

Cora let out a relieved breath.

She watched as Oggmund pulled two wrapped parcels from his inside pocket. He opened one of them to reveal a collection of bright yellow, fluffy squares.

Cora was about to ask what they were, when Tick stirred. She watched as the fairy sniffed the air loudly. And then his eyes flung open. The fairy sat up and stared at the squares in Oggmund's hand. It wasn't long until Tock was awake and sniffing the air too.

'Are they ...' began Tick.

'Where did you ...' added Tock.

'Oh, these?' replied Oggmund. The small, yellow squares in his hand glistened in the firelight. 'I found them when I was in Edor.'

'What are they?' Cora asked. She rubbed the sleep

from her eye and took a closer look. The fluffy squares
sparkled like jewels.

'Dew suckles,' said Tock quickly.

'Expensive,' added Tick.

'But delicious,' added Tock.

The fairies' eyes were locked on Oggmund's hand.

'Would you like some?' Oggmund asked, a smile
on his face.

Tock nodded enthusiastically.

Cora could see that Tick was fighting with himself
about whether to accept the food from a troll. It wasn't
long until the temptation of the sparkling treats was
too much. He nodded too.

Oggmund stood up and handed some squares to
each of them over the flames.

The dew suckle felt light in Cora's hand. She took a bite of the fluffy square. It tasted like lemons.

'What is a troll doing —' asked Tick, his mouth packed full with almost all of his dew suckles.

'Half troll,' corrected Oggmund.

Tock let out a small burp, all of his dew suckles gone. 'That was dewlicious,' said the fairy, rubbing his belly. 'Thank you.'

'What is a *half* troll doing in a cave outside of Troll Town?' Tick finished his question, having quickly swallowed his dew suckles in one giant gulp.

Oggmund opened his fur cloak and pulled out a notebook that sat inside. He held it up to them. The worn leather that held it together was cracked on the outside.

'You came all the way here to sell notebooks?' asked Tick, confused.

'Are you a travelling notebook salesman?' Tock asked.

Cora smiled at her friends as she popped another dew suckle in her mouth. Her stomach gurgled appreciatively. She had forgotten how hungry she was.

Oggmund shook his head and opened the notebook, showing them one of the pages. Drawn on the thick paper was an ogre with long, curling tusks that reached up from his mouth. Like the poster of the fairies Cora saw in Vanir, the ogre moved. He danced from one foot to the other, a large smile on his face.

Oggmund turned the page over. Drawn on the following page was a beautiful woman without any hair on her head. She twirled around in a dress that looked like it was made of scales, and Cora saw a green tail swish by her feet.

'They look almost real,' Cora said peering closer at the drawings. She rubbed her eye once more. The woman in the dress waved at her from the page.

'I've seen better,' said Tick, unimpressed.

Tock nudged his brother.

'I want to draw everyone,' said Oggmund, his face lighting up with excitement. '*All* the magical beings. Giants, witches, elves, treefolk, centaurs, necromancers, wizards, gremlins.' Oggmund stopped. 'Even … syphons.'

Cora almost choked on her dew suckle. 'Syphons?' she squeaked.

Oggmund nodded. 'Rumour has it that there's one in the northern towns,' he said. 'I'm on my way there. Imagine seeing a *real* syphon.'

Tick and Tock glanced at Cora.

'Yes,' said Tick. 'Imagine.'

'How would you know if you saw one?' Cora

asked, wondering it herself. 'They look just like everybody else, don't they?'

'Well, *I* heard they're a little smelly,' said Tick.

'And *I* heard they have webbed feet,' said Tock.

'Really?' replied Oggmund.

Cora glared at the fairies as they stifled giggles behind their hands.

'And what are you all doing here?' Oggmund asked. 'Fairies never come this far north.'

'We know,' said Tick and Tock.

Cora wasn't sure what to say. She didn't want to tell Oggmund that she was a syphon. 'We're looking for my family,' she said.

Oggmund nodded. 'Are they lost?'

Cora paused. 'You could say that,' she said, thinking of Dot. She stared into the flames of the fire. A feeling that she should be looking for Dot instead of other syphons washed over her.

'Is it because you don't have much time?' asked Oggmund.

Cora stared at the boy confused. Much time? How would he know how much time she had?

'What do you mean?' she asked, her heart beating fast.

'Until your magic takes over,' said Oggmund, 'and you become a Havoc.'

Chapter Twenty-Eight

The words from the stranger's mouth hit Cora like a bucket of cold Brolg seawater. A sharp, nervous feeling slinked between her ribs. 'How do you —' Cora began, eyes wide. How could Oggmund know? Had she said something in her dream? Was Tick right? Was Oggmund really who he said he was?

Tick flew up from the ground. 'I knew it,' said the fairy. He started grabbing their belongings. 'I told you we couldn't trust a troll.' The fairy rolled up the bedding into their packs. 'Father always said to never trust trolls.'

'He also said to never trust burnt bread,' said Tock. 'But it's still delicious.'

Cora stood up from her bedding, her mind whirring. She must have stood up too fast because she felt dizzy.

'Wait — wait,' said Oggmund, clambering up from the floor, his hands out. 'I'm sorry. I just saw …'

Then the troll stopped and pointed down to Cora's hands.

Cora followed the boy's gaze. Staring down, she could see that her hands were black. Like she had dipped them in ink. The cracks which had started on her wrists had grown so much that they now completely covered her hands.

Havoc.

She glanced at the fairies. Their faces were lined with worry.

Cora rubbed at her hands, trying to get the marks off like a stain. But they stayed right where they were — a part of her. The dizziness she felt doubled.

'Unstable magic,' said Oggmund. 'I've seen it before.'

'You have?' replied Tick. 'Where?'

Oggmund nodded. 'There was a havoc in Troll Town. Years ago.'

'What happened to them?' Cora asked.

Oggmund looked away and Cora knew all she needed to know. She was well on her way to becoming a Havoc. She didn't have much time left.

'We should go,' she said, straightening. Brushing away the dizziness, Cora helped Tock stand up from the ground. He stepped on his leg gently before flying up into the air.

'Let's find Belle. She might be able to help us,' said Tick.

Cora remembered the kind hobgoblin who had helped her with her magic before. And then she remembered what had happened to her. 'She was possessed by a warlock because of us,' said Cora, shaking her head.

'Plus she will throw vegetables at us again,' said Tock.

'I know someone who can help,' said Oggmund.

Cora stopped and looked over at the troll.

'Who?' asked Tick.

Oggmund paused. 'A troll. In Troll Town.'

Cora glanced down at her fingers. The black marks were now almost at the palms of her hands. She swallowed at the sight. Soon there wouldn't be much more of her left.

'Cora, are you alright?' asked Tock.

Cora nodded. Or at least, she thought she did. Her head felt funny. 'Where is Troll Town?' she asked.

'Not far from here,' said Oggmund.

Tick and Tock glanced at Cora.

She thought about the black cracks on her skin. The magic that had become heavier and heavier inside of her. The dreams. The voice. The way Tick and Tock looked at her since they'd found out about her missing bracelet. She had to keep going. But how long could she last? As if hearing her, the magic inside of her swirled uncomfortably. Cora thought about the princess and the Jinx in her dream. She pushed the swirling magic down.

'How do we get to Troll Town?' Cora asked.

Chapter Twenty-Nine

'Are you sure this is the right way?' Tock asked.

Tick, Tock and Cora followed Oggmund as he walked all the way into the ice cave. Each of them held a torch made from sticks and fire in their hand, their packs on their shoulders. The light from the fire torches bounced off the ice and stone walls as they moved further and further into the cave.

'It will be quicker than going around the mountain,' said Oggmund, his voice an echo in the empty and dark space ahead.

'What if it's a dead end?' Tock asked.

Oggmund stopped. He held is hand out in the air in front of him. Then he placed it on the cave wall and closed his eyes.

Cora and the fairies waited. After a moment, Cora glanced at the fairies. What was Oggmund doing?

'Trolls like caves,' whispered Tick.

'We *know* caves,' said Oggmund, his eyes still closed. 'Like fairies know food.'

If it was meant to be an insult, Tick and Tock didn't take it that way. They both smiled proudly.

Oggmund nodded, and opening his eyes, continued into the cave ahead. Cora and the fairies followed, and soon they could no longer see the morning light shining through the cave entrance behind them, glistening on the ice and stone walls. All that surrounded them and stretched out before them was darkness.

The cave floor beneath their feet slowly sloped downwards. Cora noticed that the cave walls also steadily became narrower the further they went. Soon

the space between the walls was just wide enough to fit one of them at a time.

Cora ran her hand along the sides of the cave wall. It felt cold and smooth like the wall she had lived behind in Urt.

'Watch out for shadow mites,' said Oggmund in front of her.

'Shadow mites?' Cora echoed.

'Tiny creatures,' said Tock behind her. He held his fingers apart to show how tiny. The space between his two fingers was no bigger than the size of an ant.

'They live in caves, and other dark places,' explained Oggmund.

'Sometimes in your shoes,' said Tick.

'Or your ears,' said Tock.

'They burrow under your skin,' said Tick.

'Not pleasant,' said Tock with a shake of his fairy head.

Cora pulled her hand away from the cave wall. She made sure to keep an eye out for any shadow mites and tried not to imagine them inside her ears or shoes.

'You're not from here, are you?' Oggmund asked Cora.

Cora wasn't sure what to say. She was still trying to find where she was from. She shook her head.

'She's from out of town,' added Tock.

As she walked, Cora thought about what Oggmund had said earlier about trolls *knowing* caves. She wondered what syphons knew. Were they good at navigating caves like trolls? Did they love food like fairies? Were they scavengers or collectors like Dot?

'Oggmund,' Cora said.

'Call me Ogg,' he replied.

'I prefer Oggmund,' said Tick.

'Ogg,' said Cora, ignoring the fairy. 'The rumour about syphons in the northern towns … do you know *which* of the northern towns?'

Ogg nodded. 'Tynth,' he said simply.

Tynth. Cora repeated the name of the place over and over in her head, not wanting to forget it. *Tynth.* She wondered how far away they were from it and then wished she still had Gromp's map. *Tynth*. Was Tynth where she was before Urt? Was that where she had lived with her syphon family? Cora pictured Tynth in her mind. It was beautiful like The Hollow. A quiet village filled with rolling green hills. The small, blurry memories that she had of a place before Urt filled her mind. A pair of pointed, red leather shoes in tall grass. A bright sun. Cool air on her skin. A yellow sundress. A soft laugh. *Tynth*.

'Tynth?' questioned Tock. 'Are you sure?'

Oggmund nodded.

'But nobody lives in Tynth,' said Tock.

'Tynth is not hazelnut,' said Tick.

'Habitable,' corrected Tock.

'Tynth is not habitable,' repeated Tick.

'Why not?' Cora asked.

'Father said the gas from the mud pits is poisonous to many magical creatures,' said Tock.

'Mud pits?' Cora echoed. The image she held of a beautiful place with rolling green hills and sunshine was suddenly shattered and replaced with a smelly, brown place.

Tynth.

The cave had stopped sloping and narrowing. They walked along the dark path until their torches had nearly burnt down to the ends.

'How much longer?' Tick asked.

'Can't we just magic to Troll Town?' Tock asked.

Cora remembered that she also had the witch's magic. Though she wasn't sure about using it. Her magic still flipped around inside her. The dark magic was the loudest of them all. As she felt for them, she realised that she could barely tell the magic apart.

'If you magic there, then you wouldn't be able to see this cool cave,' said Ogg with a smile.

Tick groaned.

'Plus, we don't want to draw too much attention to fairies being in Troll Town,' said Ogg.

'Should we wear disguises?' Tock suggested excitedly.

'I do a very convincing impersonation of a giant,' said Tick, puffing out his chest.

'I don't think anyone will believe that you are a giant,' said Ogg.

Cora agreed.

Then Ogg stopped. 'There's an exit up ahead,' he said.

How did he know that? Cora wondered. And then she felt it. A short breeze flew through the dark cave from somewhere she couldn't see. It must have been what Ogg felt. There was an exit close.

It wasn't long until Cora, Tick, Tock and Ogg could see light illuminating the cave up ahead. Their fires almost out, they dropped the sticks to the ground and came to a stop, at the end of the path, in front of a cave wall. The path had ended, but light still shone from somewhere.

'Dead end,' said Tick, hands on his hips.

And then Ogg pointed upwards. Light trickled down from a hole way, way up high above them.

'How do we —' Cora began, but before she could finish asking how they were going to climb to the top, two *POP!s* of magic bounced off the cave walls around them and suddenly, she was standing on the snowy outcrop of the mountain, sunlight warming her skin.

Tick and Tock had magicked them out of the cave.

'Hey,' said Ogg, disappointed.

Cora gazed out at the view from the mountain. The soft sun shone over snowy valleys and mountaintops all the way to the horizon.

Then looking down, Cora saw what lay below.

Ogg stretched his arms out. 'Troll Town.'

Chapter Thirty

Small stacked houses, some narrow and lopsided, others short and wide sat nestled below the mountain. Smoke billowed from stone chimneys on snow-covered roofs and a river turned to ice cut across the town. A large, gold bridge spanned the river. It glinted in the wintry sun.

From where she stood, Cora could see the whole town.

Magical beings dotted the streets. Some skated along the ice. Some flew what looked like kites in the air. The wind carried the smell of woodfire over to them and Cora wanted nothing more than to sit beneath a blanket in front of a fireplace somewhere, like she would do with Dot when the wind from the Urt sea chilled the wall they lived behind.

Cora pulled her coat closer against the frosty breeze.

'Now for the best part,' said Ogg with a clap of his hands. He walked over to the edge of the snowy outcrop and looked down. Then from the tall pack on his back, he pulled out a long, plastic board. He dropped it on the ground and pushed it towards the edge. The front of it tipped over the side precariously.

'Last one to the bottom is a smelly fairy!' called Ogg and then with two feet on the board, the troll pushed himself off the ledge, disappearing from sight. Cora and the fairies heard a loud 'WHOO! YEAH!' as Ogg slid down the mountainside.

'Quick,' said Tick. 'We don't want to be smelly fairies.'

With a *POP!* of magic a sleek sled appeared in front of Cora.

'But we *are* smelly fairies,' said Tock, sniffing his armpit.

'I'm not,' said Cora. She jumped on the sled and pushed it to the edge of the outcrop with her feet. She peeked over. They were high up. Very, very high up. A little too high up if you asked Cora. So, instead of standing up like Ogg, she sat down on the sled. Tick and Tock sat behind her and held on. Then taking a deep breath, Cora pushed the sled over the ledge and the three of them dove down the mountainside with a rattling speed.

Tufts of snow flew up either side of the soaring sled. They dove faster and faster. Cora held on tightly,

steering
the sled as
best as she could
down the snowy hill.
She swerved left and right
to avoid the sharp rocks that
poked out from the white blanket.

Tick and Tock shrieked with laughter as they
rocketed down the hill.

Cora grinned. The cool wind against her skin,
the soaring sled. It felt like she was flying through the
air. And for a moment, she wasn't a syphon or a Havoc.

She wasn't being chased by hunters or the council. She was just her. Just Cora. And it felt good to be just Cora. She cried out, 'WHOO! YEAH!' just like Ogg had.

'WHEEE!' cried Tick and Tock, laughing happily.

Up ahead, through the snowdrifts, Cora could see Ogg. He was already halfway down the slope, sliding and swerving around the rocks with ease.

'There he is,' said Tick, pointing to the back of the troll.

Cora couldn't help it. She reached for the princess's magic. Holding it in her grasp, she called up the cool wind around her and pushed it against the sled, moving it faster down the mountain. It was just a nudge. Just enough to catch up to Oggmund.

But she shouldn't have.

As they sped down the snowy slope, the magic inside of Cora twisted. She almost gasped as she felt it boil below her skin. She tried to pay attention, keeping her eye open as her magic fought to take control.

Suddenly, the strength of the Jinx was at her fingertips. Beneath her hands the sled cracked and buckled where she gripped it. *Oh no.* She watched wide-eyed as her magic took control. Pieces of the sled came away in her hands.

'What was that?' asked Tock, peering over her shoulder.

'N-nothing,' said Cora as she tried to get rid of the strength of the Jinx from her grip.

Then a loud rumbling noise reverberated behind them. Cora felt the sled shudder and shake beneath her hands. For a second she thought the sled had broken apart. But then she realised that it wasn't the sled that was shaking, it was the mountain.

'Uh-oh,' said Tock.

'What uh-oh?' asked Cora, unable to see behind her. She swerved, just missing a group of rocks in their path.

'An abalone!' cried Tick.

'A what?' cried Cora.

'An avalanche!' corrected Tock.

Chapter Thirty-One

Cora quickly glanced behind her. She didn't want to take her eye off the path in front of them for too long. But all she needed was a quick glance to see that barrelling towards them behind their sled was a rolling, tumbling ball of snow. It was getting bigger and bigger as it flew towards them, collecting more and more snow from the mountain with every turn.

'Uh-oh,' Cora repeated.

'Go faster!' cried Tick.

'I'm trying,' said Cora. She held onto the rollicking, speeding sled as she tried her best to shake the Jinx magic away. When it finally released her hands, Cora searched again for the princess's magic. But all the syphoned magic swirled around like smoke in a glass jar. Then black sparks flew from her fingers instead. *No, no, no.*

'Rock!' cried Tock, pointing ahead of her.

Cora almost didn't see it. She pushed the sled to

the right, skidding them out of the way just in time. The sled then spun to the left and then to the right, weaving recklessly down the slope.

Gritting her teeth, Cora tried to straighten the sled against the snow.

'It's getting closer!' said Tock.

But it was no use. The sled plummeted down the mountain. Snow flew up around the sled like a smoky white wall and Cora could no longer see where they were going. She couldn't see the rocks in her path or Ogg or even where the mountain ended.

There was a loud crack and a bump and then the sled with Tick, Tock and Cora on it flew up into the air.

'Argh!' they all cried.

And for a moment, Cora could see in front of her. They weren't far from the bottom of the mountain. And she could see Ogg, waiting for them.

The sled landed back down on the slope with a rough bang and a jolt. They had hit a rock. Cora straightened the sled but it shot to the left, skidding diagonally across the snow. Without her magic, there wasn't much left she could do. Cora felt herself losing control of the sled. She gritted her teeth as they hit more and more rocks. She just needed to keep the sled steady for a little bit longer. They veered and skidded across the snow, zigzagging perilously down the slope.

'Hold on!' Cora cried out.

With a lurch and a bump they reached the bottom of the mountain. The sled spun across the snow, almost toppling over. It swivelled in a circle along the icy floor.

'ARGH!' Cora, Tick and Tock cried as they spun around and around and around across the slippery icy surface like a spinning top.

When the sled came to a stop, the three of them jumped up. Dizzy, they stumbled.

'I think I'm going to be sick,' moaned Tick and he grabbed his belly.

'GO, GO!' cried Cora to the fairies.

The fairies flew ahead as Cora raced behind them. She could hear the rumbling of snow getting louder and louder. The avalanche sounded like it was almost on top of them. She sprinted after the fairies, not daring to look back.

Ahead of them, Ogg stood calmly, his arms crossed.

'What are you doing?!' Cora asked. 'There's an avalanche!' She pointed behind her. She grabbed onto the troll's arm and tried to pull him with her as they darted away from the mountain.

But Ogg stood where he was, unmoving. And then he laughed. 'That's not an avalanche,' he said. 'That's Martin.'

Martin? Cora stopped running and pulling the half troll by the arm.

'Martin?' echoed Tick and Tock fluttering to a stop in mid-air.

Ogg pointed behind them, a small smile on his face.

Cora peered behind her, entirely expecting to see a large unstoppable wall of snow barrelling towards them. But as she looked on, she watched the rolling ball of snow come to a stop at the bottom of the mountain. And then it ... sprung open. The ball of snow was actually a pair of arms, legs, a body and a head. It was a magical being.

Cora stared open-mouthed as the ball of snow got to its feet. The ground rumbled as he stretched upwards. Standing high above them, a large toothy smile spread across its face.

'A snow giant,' said Tock in awe.

Ogg was right. It wasn't an avalanche at all.

Cora tilted her head up to look at Martin. He was almost half the size of the mountain they had slid down. The ginormous snow giant was covered in fluffy, white fur, his smiling, friendly face gazing down at them.

Then the giant shook the excess snow from his white fur. Clumps of snow flung their way, splattering each of them.

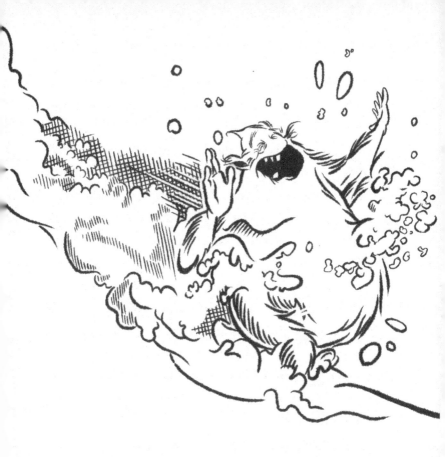

'Oh,' said Cora, wiping the snow from her cheeks.

'He just wanted to join in,' said Ogg.

'Hi Martin,' said Tick, waving, his face almost entirely covered in snow.

Martin held up a hand to the fairy.

'There aren't many snow giants around anymore,' said Tock.

'Why not?' Cora asked. She thought about syphons. Were snow giants hunted and killed too?

'There's not a lot of room for them,' said Ogg. 'They only have these mountains. And many think that they're dangerous.'

Cora watched as the snow giant lumbered past them. In one giant step, Martin stepped over half of Troll Town, and then careful not to disrupt the town beneath his feet, Martin headed towards the much bigger mountain that sat on the other side of Troll Town.

The magic inside of Cora stirred. She stopped. Closing her eye, she tried to will it away. She felt it roll around inside her like Martin rolled down the mountain. The unstable magic was getting stronger, bigger. Opening her eye, she looked down at her hands. They were now covered entirely. They weren't hers anymore.

'Are you alright Cora?' Tick asked, the fairies flying to her side.

Cora nodded. Though she didn't think so.

'This way,' said Ogg.

Chapter Thirty-Two

Cora, Tick and Tock followed Ogg into Troll Town. Not wanting to attract attention, Tick and Tock fluttered to the ground and walked by her side.

'How is your leg?' Cora asked Tock.

'Almost back to normal,' said Tock. He bent his leg back and forth, showing her. 'See?'

Cora was thankful they had found Oggmund when they did. She made sure to keep an eye out for Rumple Leaves. Just in case.

Oggmund led them towards the main street before turning sharply down a path hidden between a house with no windows and a shop with a very slanted door. One by one, they squeezed down the path, which led onto another street that was humming with trolls and other magical beings.

Nearby, young trolls played in the snow. Some built snowmen in the shape of trolls. With rocks for eyes and leaves for hair, the snow trolls waddled down the street, chasing after the young trolls who giggled with laughter.

'Troll magic,' said Tick.

'Not all trolls have it,' said Tock.

Another group of trolls were throwing snowballs at each other. Cora watched as some of the snow shot around corner, into windows, and up and around in the air like they had minds of their own. Cora saw one snowball even hover in the air, waiting patiently for the troll child to peek out from her hiding place beneath a flight of stairs.

They ducked down another path that led away from the busy street. As they moved around the houses and shops, a strong smell filled the air. It smelt like meat and something else Cora couldn't quite put her finger on.

'Troll stew,' said Tock, also sniffing the air.

'Father says it's made with toes,' said Tick.

'Tongues, actually,' said Ogg.

Tick's and Tock's eyes widened.

Ogg laughed. 'Kidding.'

They snuck through Troll Town, Ogg peering around corners to make sure the trolls were far enough away. They walked behind houses and between buildings until eventually Cora found herself staring up at the very large, very gold bridge. It arched above them like a shining jewel.

Beneath it lay the iced-over river Cora had seen from high on the mountain, and on top of the ice, trolls played. Some skated along it, spinning and jumping in the air. Others sat on it, and some even lay sleeping on the ice. Every now and then, Cora saw a troll glide across the snow on a board like Ogg's. Laughter peppered the air.

Ogg, Tick and Tock took a right turn ahead but Cora stayed where she was. She watched, her eye transfixed on the skating trolls. For a moment, Cora wanted to join them. She had never skated on ice before. She had never even seen snow or ice before yesterday, now that she thought about it. At least, not that she could remember.

A troll family shot around the ice. The troll boy slipped and slid clumsily as he skated after his parents.

'Cora?' called Ogg.

Cora turned and saw the fairies and Ogg waiting for her by the side of a house shaped like a stack of pancakes. She looked back at the family of ice-skating trolls once more. And then she turned and followed the others down another hidden path.

At the end of the narrow path, Ogg glanced around the corner of a shop and motioned for them to follow him when the street was clear. When he stepped out into the street, a voice called out to him.

'Ogg?'

Tick, Tock and Cora stopped. They stayed hidden in the shadows of the shop.

Ogg froze in place

'Ogg?' came the voice again. 'Is that you?'

The troll glanced back at them with a look that said *stay there*. Then Ogg slowly turned around.

Cora, Tick and Tock could see an older troll standing in the middle of the empty street. She had a cane in her hand and her long, grey hair was tied in many plaits. Each plait glinted with a strand of gold.

'What are you doing back here?' the older troll asked. 'I thought you were on your big adventure?'

'I am, Your Majesty,' said Ogg in a small bow. 'I have just, um … forgotten something.'

'Oh no,' said Tick. 'That's her?'

'Who?' asked Cora.

'The Troll Queen,' whispered Tock.

The older troll didn't look like any queen Cora had ever seen. But then again, she had never seen a queen before.

'Martin said he saw you on the mountain,' the Troll Queen said. Then her eyes shifted to glance

behind Ogg and rest right where Cora, Tick and Tock stood hidden.

The three of them quickly ducked lower behind the shop wall.

Cora watched Ogg nod in response. And then the Troll Queen said something else to Ogg but they couldn't hear what it was.

With one last glance in their direction, the Troll Queen walked away from Ogg and after two steps, she disappeared in a flurry of snow.

Cora, Tick and Tock stepped out from their hiding spot and walked over to Ogg.

'That was close,' said Ogg. 'We're almost there.'

Cora was relieved. She had started to feel dizzy again.

The four of them turned down a side street and came to a stop outside a small shop. The store was lopsided, its roof bent under the weight of the snow on top. A sign hung from the stone door. It said CLOTHED.

Cora thought it might have meant CLOSED.

'Let me do the talking,' said Ogg, before pushing the door open. The three of them followed, stepping inside the lopsided shop.

Chapter Thirty-Three

Inside the shop, it was darker than Cora expected. The walls, ceiling and floor were all made from a glinting grey stone. Lanterns that flickered yellow and red were bolted into the stone. The light bounced off the stone, giving the shop a soft, amber glow. It was like they had stepped inside a cave.

The warmth inside the shop felt nice on Cora's skin. Looking around, she noticed by the window a chair was being carved out of stone, but not by someone. The chisel floated in the air by itself, tap-tapping against the stone.

Stone tables, vases and lamps filled the shop floor, each of them made out of different coloured stone. Some were so shiny Cora could see her reflection staring back at her. She paused as she peered into a glimmering purple bowl. She almost didn't recognise the girl who stared back. Her eye was sunken, her skin pale.

In front of them, standing behind a red stone counter in the middle of the shop was a very large troll. He was much taller and wider than Ogg, in fact, he was at least double the half troll's size. The shopkeeper wore a green hat that was much too small for his head, and in the amber light, Cora could see that the shopkeeper's skin was deep blue.

'Yoohoo!' the troll shopkeeper called out. He waved to them from behind the counter. Behind the shopkeeper troll sat a collection of hammers, chisels, screws and bolts. They hung from the wall and Cora noticed that each one of them jiggled and bounced on its hook.

Ogg approached the counter and the three friends followed.

'Yoohoo, Ogg —' began the shopkeeper. He stopped when his eyes settled on Tick and Tock. His cheery smile fell from his face faster than a dropped plate.

'Fairies!' the shopkeeper said, recoiling.

'Dimm,' said Ogg, holding up his hands. 'We need your help.'

'*Help?*' echoed the shopkeeper. 'Yes, you do need help, Oggmund. Why are you here with fairies? And why are fairies in Troll Town? And why are fairies in my shop? Fairies!'

The shopkeeper peered at Tick and Tock suspiciously.

It was an odd sight to Cora, to see such a large troll so frightened of two plump and hairy fairies like Tick and Tock.

'It's a long story,' said Ogg. 'We need to see your brother.'

'He's busy,' said Dimm. But even Cora could see that the troll was not telling the whole truth. His eyes remained glued to Tick and Tock.

'Dimm,' said Ogg, 'you can trust me.'

Dimm shifted his weight from one foot to the other, thinking. 'What — what if they steal something?' Dimm asked, grabbing the nearest thing to him. He held it against his chest protectively. It was a wrench.

'We don't want that,' said Tock, making a face at the wrench.

'We don't know where it's been,' said Tick, also making a face.

'And fairies don't *steal*,' said Tock.

'We *borrow*,' said Tick, proudly.

Cora rolled her eyes.

As if seeing her for the first time, the troll shopkeeper's eyes fell on her. And then on her hands.

'You're ...' Dimm said, pointing.

Instinctively, Cora pushed her hands behind her back. 'Hopefully, not yet,' she said.

They waited patiently for the shopkeeper to make up his mind. Her head had begun to pound. Instead of recoiling in fear like he had done with the fairies, Dimm the shopkeeper troll looked down at her, understanding in his eyes.

'Please,' Tock said.

'We won't stea — *borrow* anything,' said Tick. 'We promise.'

The fairy held out his pinky finger in the air.

Dimm stared at it, uncertain. Then, the shopkeeper troll grabbed onto Tick's pinky with his large hand and shook it.

Then the shopkeeper looked at Ogg and nodded. 'He's downstairs.'

Dimm motioned to the floor near a wall that held very large stone spoons. And Cora saw for the first time a set of stairs carved into the floor. From where she stood, she could see an amber glow shining up from below. The stairs led down to another room.

Ogg walked down the steps first and Cora, Tick and Tock followed.

At the bottom of the stone steps, the four of them entered a room that looked exactly like the one they had just left. Cora paused. And then blinked. Just like upstairs, nearby a stone chair was being carved by a floating chisel, there were stone tables, bowls, lamps and vases set up across the floor.

'Yoohoo!' said a troll by a red stone counter in the middle of the room. He looked exactly the same as Dimm the shopkeeper.

'Is that …' began Cora, wondering if Dimm had magicked his way down the stairs faster than they had walked.

'This is Dimm's brother, Dunn,' said Ogg.

Dunn the troll waved to them.

They waved back before following Ogg down another set of stone steps in the floor. Like the ones before, the stairs descended down into another amber-lit space. And again, Cora, Tick and Tock found themselves in a room that matched the previous two. Cora wondered how far down the shop went.

'Yoohoo!' said a troll from behind a red counter in the middle of the room.

And how many brothers Dimm the shopkeeper actually had.

'Is this him?' asked Tock.

'No, this is Dimm and Dunn's brother, Dinn.'

The troll waved to them.

They waved back and followed Ogg down another set of stone stairs in the floor. The steps led to another room that was exactly the same as the first three rooms.

'Is this him?' asked Tick.

'No, this is Dimm, Dunn and Dinn's sister, Donn,' Ogg said.

Cora, Tick and Tock paused.

'Yoohoo!' said Donn the shopkeeper. She waved at them from another red stone counter.

They waved back and followed Ogg down the next set of stone stairs. When they reached the bottom, Cora was relieved to find that the room they entered didn't match all the others. There were no vases, or tables, or a floating chisel tap-tapping away at a stone chair. Instead, the room was covered in … rocks. Baskets full of them sat on the floor. Some rocks weren't in baskets at all, and sat haphazardly in lumpy piles. Cora saw a few of the rocks glinted and sparkled different colours. In the corner of the room, a large metal furnace sat open and inside it was a roaring blue fire. It sent a wave of heat towards them, so hot, Cora had to look away.

Standing behind yet another red counter was a troll who looked exactly like the other troll shopkeepers, except that he wore a soot-stained apron, and a small glass monocle sat over one of his eyes. He glanced up at them from a messy stack of papers. 'Oggmund!' he said.

'Dann,' said Ogg. 'The best stonemaker in all of
Troll Town.'

'I'm the *only* stonemaker in all of Troll Town,' said
Dann with a low chuckle. 'What are you doing here?
I thought you were on your adventure?'

'I was,' said Ogg. 'But there is someone I want you
to meet.'

'I've met fairies before, Ogg,' said Dann, eyeing Tick and Tock.

'Not like us, you haven't,' said Tock.

Cora had to agree.

Then Dann looked over at Cora, his eyes shifting from her hair, to her missing eye and then down to her hands.

'Ogg,' said Dann warningly. He shook his head.

'Dann, please,' said Ogg.

'We don't have much time,' said Tock. 'The council …'

'The council?' Dann questioned.

'They may or may not be looking for us,' said Tick.

'You must have upset them terribly,' said Dann with a chuckle.

'We *might* have borrowed something,' said Tock.

Magic. And it was more stolen than borrowed, Cora thought. She wished she could give all of the magic she had absorbed back. If only she knew how.

'Dann,' said Ogg, 'I promised we could help. She is different.'

The troll peered at Cora. She shifted her feet under his scrutinising gaze.

'I've never really liked the council,' said Dann. And then he stopped and looked around the room, as if he were waiting for something to happen, a consequence for uttering the words. And when nothing did, he relaxed. 'How old are you?' he asked, looking at her through his monocle.

'Eleven,' said Cora.

'Eleven years old, one eye, wanted by the council and on the verge of becoming a Havoc,' said Dann. 'That *is* different.'

Chapter Thirty-Four

Dann lifted one of his hands and a stone chair slid across the floor from behind the red counter. It swivelled and turned, scraping against the stone floor until it came to a stop behind Cora.

'Please, sit,' the troll said.

Cora sat down in the chair. It was cold to the touch and not very comfortable.

'How long since the symptoms began?' Dann asked.

'Uh, I'm not sure,' said Cora. She thought back to Jade City, when Archibald Drake melted her bracelet. 'A few days?'

Dann glanced at Ogg.

'This is very advanced for just a few days,' said Dann. 'Are you sure?'

Cora nodded.

Dann stepped out from behind the counter. He gazed at her closely through his glass monocle. The

small piece of round glass in front of his eye shrunk and grew on his face.

'Can you please show me your teeth?' Dann asked.

'My teeth?' replied Cora.

The troll nodded.

Hesitantly, Cora opened her mouth wide. She had never shown anyone inside her mouth before. Not since that time Dot took her temperature one winter, years ago.

Cora watched as the troll used a small smooth stick to peek inside. Then Tick's and Tock's heads came into view next to him as they looked inside too. Ogg did the same.

'Ah-ha,' said Tock, nodding. 'Just as I suspected. She has teeth.'

'Are you brushing them twice a day?' asked Tick.

Dann shook his head at the fairies before stepping away from Cora. She closed her mouth.

'And where are you cracking?' asked the troll.

Cora held out her hands. She pulled back her sleeves to show the troll the black cracks that reached from her hands all the way up to her shoulders.

'Nightmares?' Dann asked.

Cora nodded.

'Sleepwalking?'

Cora nodded.

'And she snores,' added Tick.

'And twitches in her sleep,' said Tock.

Ogg smirked.

Cora glared at the fairies.

'What?' Tick asked, holding his hands up innocently.

'It could be helpful for him to know,' added Tock with a smile.

'It's not,' said Dann. 'Magic?' he asked.

Cora tore her glaring eyes from the fairies. 'Pardon?'

'What magic is causing the cracking?' asked Dann. 'Are you a witch? An ogre? You're certainly not hairy enough to be a fairy.'

'A mage? A necromancer?' added Ogg.

'The last creature that came through the shop was a ghoul,' said Dann. 'He kept turning invisible. It was very difficult to keep track of where he floated.'

Cora looked at Tick and Tock. Then she glanced at Ogg. Should she tell the trolls that she was a syphon? She paused, unsure. The trolls were helping her. She could trust them, couldn't she? And then before she knew it, the word tumbled from her mouth. 'Syphon.'

There was silence. Cora watched Dann's eyes grow wide as he leant back against the red counter.

Ogg stared at her, his mouth open. Then he scrambled for something inside his coat pocket.

'Can I ...' Ogg began, pulling out his notebook and pen. Cora remembered what he had said in the cave about syphons. He wanted to draw her.

Cora hesitated before nodding.

'That explains how advanced your symptoms are. How much magic do you have?' asked Dann.

Cora counted up the different magics she had absorbed since she left Urt. The Jinx. Princess Avette. The warlock. The witch. And the one that she didn't know. 'Five,' she said.

Dann nodded.

'Can you help her?' Tick asked.

'You need ice stone,' said the troll. 'True ice stone is very rare. It's found in the furthest regions, in the deepest caves on the highest mountain peaks. It would take weeks to find enough stones,' said Dann, shaking his head. Then he looked at Cora. 'You do not have weeks.'

Cora swallowed. The words repeated themselves in her mind. *You do not have weeks.* She thought of Dot and Scratch. And her syphon family.

'And there are only a few trolls who know how to make ice stone,' added Dann.

Cora, Tick and Tock waited for Dann to finish. Was he one of them? Ogg had said he was the best stonemaker in Troll Town.

Dann stared back at them. 'Obviously, I am one of them.'

Cora felt herself sigh in relief.

'It won't be as strong,' said Dann. 'But it might work.'

Cora nodded. She was happy with *might*. 'Thank you,' she said. Tick and Tock nodded.

Dann walked over to one of the boxes filled with rocks that sat about the room. He held onto one and shuffled through the rocks inside. He peered at some, turning them in his hands, before setting a few aside. Then walking back to the counter, he pulled out a glass case. Opening it, Cora saw brilliant sparkling stones of different shapes and sizes. Dann grabbed a black one, a white one and a red one and placed them into a giant bowl with a collection of other glinting grey rocks.

Cora recognised two of the stones. The black one was identical to the one that sat in a ring Archibald Drake wore. And the white stone, she had seen in Jade City before they met Artemis.

'Heart stone,' said Cora, remembering what the stone was called. She remembered it because the small markings etched on the stone were the same as those etched onto the spellbox she had found in Urt. The one that had contained the Jinx curse.

Dann nodded. 'And obsidian stone. And fire stone. The three most powerful stones in the kingdom, besides ice stone.'

Dann picked up the bowl and walked over to the furnace. He placed a pair of goggles over his eyes and put the bowl into the fiery chamber. Then he took out a very large, red stone pot. He closed the door and turned back to them. 'Now, we wait.' He placed the giant bowl on the counter and Cora could smell what it was immediately. The smell that now filled the room was the same smell that had filled their noses when they had entered Troll Town.

'Troll stew,' said Dann proudly. He waved a hand and out flew five stone bowls from behind a pile of rocks.

The stew smelt delicious.

'And by *wait* do you mean *eat*?' Tick asked, unable to stop himself from peering into the steaming pot.

Dann served a helping of stew to each of them and himself.

Without waiting for it to cool, both of the fairies found themselves a pile of rocks to sit on and began slurping up the hot troll stew.

Then Tock stopped suddenly. 'Are there toes in this?' he asked.

'What?' replied Dann.

'Never mind,' said Tock and continued eating the stew.

Cora watched as Ogg and Dann did the same and soon the room was full of hungry stew slurps. She blew on her hot stew before lifting the bowl to her mouth and tasting it. The brown soup was warm and full to the brim with vegetables. Dot would have approved.

When they had slurped their bowls clean, Tick and Tock lay down on their pile of rocks. And Ogg went back to drawing in his notebook. Every so often he glanced up at her, his brow furrowed in concentration.

'It was the trolls who helped the syphons, you know,' said Dann to Cora. 'In the beginning. For many years, our family mined the stones in these mountains.'

'Have you ever met a syphon?' Cora asked, hopeful. She took another gulp of the warm stew as she waited to hear the troll's answer.

Dann nodded his head slowly.

Cora inched forward in her seat. At last. Someone who could talk to her about syphons. Cora thought of her family. Had they come here? Had they visited Troll Town? Did Dann know them?

'But that was many years ago,' said Dann, shaking his head. 'You're the first syphon I have met in a long, long time.'

Cora tried not to let it show on her face, but with the troll's words, the hope she had felt suddenly flew from her like a snowflake in the wind.

Chapter Thirty-Five

Cora tried to shake away what she was feeling but it stuck to her like a sticky plumdrop. 'Do you know what happened to them?' she asked.

The troll placed his bowl of troll stew down on the counter. 'The ice stone protected them from themselves ... but not from others,' he said.

Hunted and killed, Cora remembered. She could see sadness flicker in the troll's eyes as he looked away from his bowl of stew.

'And then they all just ...' the troll stopped. 'Disappeared.'

'Disappeared?' echoed Ogg, glancing up from his notebook. 'Like magic?'

Cora hadn't thought of that. Is that what had happened to the syphons? They had used magic to escape?

'Some say they got hold of a strong magic, yes,' said Dann. 'One that could hide all of them, an entire community for years and years. Hide them away from anyone. Away from those wanting to find them.'

Deep down, Cora hoped that was the case. Though she wondered how she would ever find her syphon family if it were true. A sadness slunk inside her. And if they hid themselves away … *why didn't they take me with them?*

'That kind of magic could only be dark magic,' said Dann. 'Dark magic can have … repercussions.'

'Repercussions?' echoed Cora.

'Some say the magic they used to hide themselves, also destroyed them,' said Dann.

'But — but they wouldn't have had a choice,' Cora said. 'If they were being hunted and killed.' She thought of Archibald Drake, and the dark magic she took from him. She peered at her cracking hands. *Repercussions.*

Dann nodded. 'Dark magic can destroy many things. Even sometimes the magical beings who wield it.'

Cora looked over at Tick and Tock. The fairies stared at her knowingly.

'Others say,' continued Dann, 'that there were simply no syphons left alive. That other magical beings had destroyed every last one of them.'

'What do you believe?' Cora asked.

'Well,' said Dann, 'a few hours ago, I believed there were no longer any syphons left.' Then the troll met her eyes, locking onto them with a firm gaze. 'And then an eleven-year-old girl with one eye walked through the shop door.'

Tick, Tock, Ogg and Dann stared at Cora. The room fell silent.

'There were rumours of syphons in the northern towns,' Cora said, disrupting the heavy silence.

Dann nodded. 'I heard them. Is that where you are going?'

Cora, Tick and Tock nodded.

'What if they don't want to be found?' asked Dann.

The troll's words dropped like stones into Cora's stomach. Cora hadn't thought of that. What if they didn't want to be found? What if finding the syphons put them in danger?

Dann held up his hand and a pair of gloves floated over to him. The troll went back to the furnace and pulling on the gloves, he reached inside and took out the bowl of stones and rocks.

Black smoke billowed out from the top of the bowl as he placed it on the counter. Sitting up in her chair, Cora looked inside it. All of the stones had completely melted, creating a shimmering liquid at the bottom of the bowl.

Dann waved his hand over the bowl. The bowl moved, swirling the liquid round and round. Cora watched it change colour from black, to red, to silver, to white. And then the bowl stopped moving, but the liquid didn't. It turned by itself, spinning and folding into itself inside the bowl.

Then Dann pulled out a bucket of ice. Carefully, he poured the shimmering, thick liquid over the ice in the shape of a circle. It sizzled and white smoke flew up into the air. Then with his gloves still on, Dann waved a hand over the circle. It split apart in three pieces and Cora watched amazed as it wove itself together. The firm liquid braided each of its strands intricately, one on top of the next. Over, under, over, under, until at last it formed a round, white chain. A necklace.

Dann motioned to Cora. 'Try it on.'

Tick and Tock fluttered over to the counter and Ogg stopped drawing.

Cora hesitated. Carefully, she reached down into the bucket and touched the newly formed necklace. It was as cold as the ice it sat on. Picking it up, she held it in her hands and looked at it closely. It wasn't as bright as her ice-stone bracelet, but it was close. It glinted in her hands.

Cora reached up and placed the necklace over her head. She closed her eye and waited. She felt Tick,

Tock, Ogg and Dann waiting too. She waited to feel something. For the rumbling of magic inside her to become quiet. For the heaviness she felt to lift. Seconds turned into minutes and then when minutes went by, and nothing happened, Cora opened her eye. She stared down at her cracking hands. They were still the same.

'Give it time,' said Dann.

Cora nodded. 'How can we ever repay you?' she asked. She thought about what she had. A pair of clothes. A jar of gooseberry honey. Dot's pocket watch.

Dann looked over at Ogg.

'Take him with you,' said Dann.

Ogg's eyes lit up.

Cora glanced at Tick and Tock. She could tell by the looks on the fairies faces that they weren't thrilled about the troll joining them.

'You might need a troll where you're going,' said Dann.

'Half troll,' Ogg said, but he puffed his chest out all the same. Then he faltered. 'Mother will never allow it, Uncle Dann.'

'Trolls need adventure. *Real* adventure,' said Dann.

Tick and Tock stroked their chins in thought.

'Do you have any more of those delicious dew suckles?' asked Tick.

Ogg nodded.

Tick and Tock smiled happily.

They said their goodbyes to Dann and after climbing up all of the steps through all of the levels of the shop and waving to all of Dann's siblings, Cora, Tick, Tock and Ogg, stepped outside into the snowy Troll Town street.

Not wanting anyone to see it, Cora tucked the ice-stone necklace beneath her clothes. The sharp chill of the necklace hit Cora's skin like a splash of water.

'Here,' said Ogg. He turned and handed her his open notebook.

Drawn delicately onto the rough paper was a portrait of Cora. Standing alone on the page, the drawn Cora smiled back at her. She wasn't pale. Her eye wasn't sunken or dark. Her hands and arms weren't cracked. She looked like herself. She looked perfectly ordinary.

'What do you think?' Ogg asked.

Cora was speechless.

'You forgot the stink lines,' said Tick, peering at the drawing.

Tock giggled.

They made their way down the street, Cora's eye on the drawing. Then a cool wind blew the pages over in her hands. The pages flipped past and Cora saw the amazing creatures that filled Ogg's notebook. Dwarves, elves, nymphs, ghouls. She turned the pages. Fauns, pixies. There were so many. And then Cora came to a page that made her stop in her tracks. Her heart jumped up into her chest as she gazed down at the page. On it was a drawing of someone she had seen many times before. Someone with hair that was sharp like knives, and a dark, hollow stare.

Chapter Thirty-Six

*C*ora almost dropped the notebook in her hands.

'What is it?' asked Tock.

'Is it a drawing of us?' asked Tick. 'Do I look prettier than Tock?'

'Hairier, maybe,' said Tock, sticking his tongue out.

Cora felt her skin go cold as she stared down at the image scratched onto the page. The drawing was of a crowd of magical folk and amongst them, staring back at her … was the silver-haired man. He moved, half hidden amongst a crowd but to Cora, he stood out like a silver moon in the night sky.

'Whe-where did you …' she began, unable to take her eyes from Ogg's drawing.

Tick and Tock flew over to her.

'Is that …' added Tock.

Cora nodded. She held up the notebook to Ogg, showing him the drawing.

'What?' asked Ogg. 'You don't like it? I thought it was some of my best work.'

'It's not that,' said Cora. 'Where did you see him?' she pointed to the man in the crowd.

The fairies fluttered next to her and crossed their arms seriously.

'And when?' asked Tick.

'I–I don't know. A few days ago,' said Ogg. 'In Edor. Why?'

'What was he doing? Where was he going? Did you talk to him?' Cora asked.

Ogg shook his head.

Cora looked at Tick and Tock.

'But he was with someone else,' said Ogg. 'I think I drew him too. A strange-looking man.'

Ogg took the notebook and flipped through the pages, stopping at one of them. 'Him,' he said pointing to the page. He handed the notebook back to Cora and the fairies.

Drawn in rough black lines on the page was a man with long, dark hair that greyed at the sides. He was standing on a street corner, wearing a familiar cloak and boots. His face looked like it was stretched uncomfortably across his bones. Annoyance flickered in his eyes, and his mouth was set in a permanent grim line. An obsidian ring glinted from his hand.

It was Archibald Drake. The warlock.

'But …' breathed Cora. 'The Jinx.'

She remembered watching the warlock get thrown across Jade City by the Jinx.

'Are you sure they were with each other?' Cora asked.

Ogg nodded.

Archibald Drake and the silver-haired man. Was the silver-haired man working with the warlock? If Archibald knew she was a syphon … did that mean the silver-haired man knew too? Flashes of Princess Avette's memory entered her mind. The lightning. Feathers spattered with blood. Screams. The echo of an evil laugh.

'Maybe they're both warlocks?' Tock suggested.

'Warlocks do like to calculate,' said Tick, thinking.

'Congregate,' corrected Tock.

'They do like to congregate,' said Tick.

A group of trolls entered the street where Cora and her friends stood. They came out of one of the shops chatting loudly about the price of cabbage.

Ogg, Tick, Tock and Cora quickly ducked out of the street and hid in the shadows of a narrow path between two homes.

'Who is Archibald Drake?' Ogg asked as he led the way down the path. Cora handed the notebook to Ogg and he placed it back inside his coat.

'Archibald Drake is a warlock,' said Tock.

'He's mean, scary and dangerous,' said Tick.

'He knows that I'm a syphon,' said Cora. 'And tried to kill us in Jade City.'

'Oh,' said Ogg.

'The other man,' Cora stopped. How could she explain the silver-haired man? She thought of Princess Avette, Artemis and the avian kingdom. 'We're not so sure who or what he is,' Cora said.

'But we know he is also mean, scary and dangerous,' added Tick.

'He destroyed a kingdom ... and a princess,' said Cora.

'Oh,' said Ogg again.

'Ogg, how far away is Edor?' Cora asked fearfully.

'Not far,' said Ogg.

Cora blanched. The thought of Archibald Drake and the silver-haired man being nearby made her skin crawl.

'Maybe if we find the silver-haired man, the council will forget that you're a syphon who syphoned their magic?' Tick suggested.

'Doubtful,' said Tock. 'We should stay away from Edor.'

Cora had to agree with Tock. The further they stayed away from the two men the better. She just hoped that the two of them weren't looking for the same thing they were.

'But ... the dew suckles,' said Tick mournfully.

The narrow path ended and the three friends and Ogg stepped around a corner into another street.

'I can't believe it. A *real* adventure,' Ogg said happily. 'Many trolls tell stories of their adventures. Of dragons! And hidden treasures! I've never been allowed —'

Then Ogg came to a sudden stop in the snow-covered lane.

Ahead of them, Cora saw a woman step out from the shadows. She walked out into the centre of the street and stopped. Her eyes on them.

Cora's stomach backflipped as she recognised who it was. The woman had yellow hair. And hands that glowed red like fire.

The syphon hunter.

She had found them.

Chapter Thirty-Seven

'Hunters!' said Tick and Tock.

'This way,' said Ogg. He darted across the lane and into a side street nearby.

Cora didn't hesitate. She turned on her heel and ran after the troll. The fairies weren't far behind. They sent sparks of fairy magic at the hunter before zooming after Cora and Ogg.

Crates, boxes, sleds, shoes all shot up from where they lay in the street and came soaring towards them, glowing red. They crashed against the walls of shops, missing their heads as the friends darted down the side street.

Running down the path, Ogg raced ahead and Cora did the same. Heart thumping, she glanced down at her hands. They were still cracked. The last time she had used the unstable warlock magic she had ended up possessing the magical being.

The four of them shot in and out of tiny streets.

Sliding and sprinting as fast as they could around corners, hoping to lose the hunter on their tail. With every corner they turned, flying objects crashed against the walls behind them, narrowly missing them.

Cora saw more trolls start to appear in the streets as they ran down them.

'Go, run!' Cora cried out to them, hoping they would go in the opposite direction to the woman with glowing hands or take shelter in some of the shops.

But the trolls just stared back at her, some trolls stopped. Others pointed. And some recoiled at the sight of Tick and Tock fluttering past.

Ogg skidded around a corner. Cora was close behind him, her boots sliding in the slippery snow. As they dove into the street, they collided with a pair of trolls and tumbled to the ground. The pair of trolls toppled with them to the floor.

'Sorry!' said Cora.

'Sorry!' said Ogg, helping the trolls to their feet.

'That's alright — ah! Fairies!' said one of the trolls as she jumped back at the sight of the fluttering Tick and Tock. 'Shoo!' she said, waving her hand at them.

'We will not,' said Tock.

'Wait a minute,' said the other troll. 'Aren't you three those —'

But whatever the troll was going to say, they didn't hear it. A pile of skates on the ground glowed red with the hunter's magic. The skates lifted up into the air, but before they could be flung in their direction, Ogg grabbed Cora's hand and the four of them barrelled down the street at high speed, turning down another narrow pathway.

They weaved in and out of trolls and magical beings as they filled the streets. It looked like Ogg was leading them closer and closer towards the centre of Troll Town. Some creatures saw them coming and moved out of their way until Ogg finally steered them down a short road hidden from view behind a pie shop.

Ogg slowed, and happy with the distance they had put between themselves and the hunter, they stopped.

Cora put her hands on her knees and tried to catch her breath. 'How did they find us?' she asked Tick and Tock as they fluttered in the air next to her.

'Some hunters use tracking spells,' said Ogg, panting. 'Did they touch any of you?'

Cora, Tick and Tock shook their heads.

'Do you have anything of theirs?' asked Ogg.

Cora thought back to what had happened when the hunters found them in the grass field. She remembered the warlock magic taking control and

that she had accidentally possessed the hunter. That …
and the dart in Tock's leg.

'The only thing I can think of …' Cora stopped
and looked at Tock.

The fairy smiled sheepishly.

'Don't tell me you kept it,' said Cora, eyes wide.

Slowly, Tock pulled the dart out from his pack.

'Tock!' said Tick.

'What? It's a souvenir,' said the fairy defensively.

Tick tried to grab the dart from Tock, but the
fairy held it up high out of his brother's reach.

'A souvenir that's going to get us killed,' said Ogg.
'Or worse.'

'Give it, Tock,' said Tick. He finally wrestled the
dart away from his brother. Then, flying up high
into the air, Tick threw the dart as far in the opposite
direction as he could. It skated and bounced across the
roofs of the shops and houses in the street.

Tock crossed his arms and mumbled an apology.

'We need to keep moving,' said Cora.

Having caught their breath, they walked to the
end of the narrow path and onto the street in front
of them. The street opened up into a wide square. It
looked like they had reached the Troll Town square.

Ogg turned to the fairies. 'You might need to
blend in.'

Tick and Tock flew to the ground and scrunched up their faces. They walked back and forth, slow and hunched over like they were looking for something on the ground.

Cora raised an eyebrow at them.

'These are our troll faces,' said Tick, peering up at Cora and Ogg through squinting eyes.

'And our troll walk,' said Tock, hunching over even more.

Ogg shrugged and together they entered the Troll Town square. Shops sat around the edges of the square, which was crowded with trolls and other magical folk. Some trolls skated past on the snow on boards like Ogg's and glowing skates. Some pulled other trolls or their purchases on sleds behind them.

Trolls called out to passersby in the square, selling items Cora had never seen before. One troll sold exploding earwax. It cracked and popped next to him. Another troll sold talking tambourines.

'What fine weather we have today,' the box of tambourines said as she passed them. 'Did you see the score of the big game? Should you be wearing that hat?'

Tick paused in thought by a troll selling hiccup berries before Tock dragged him away.

Cora glanced into a few of the shops to her left. One sold floating stew pots, and another had wooden troll dolls in the window. The troll dolls turned their heads and blinked at her as she walked past.

Cora looked over her shoulder. She searched the crowd and square for any sign of the woman chasing them. When she heard a loud *whoosh* above her, she peered up into the sky, searching it with her eye. It had sounded like gliding wings. But she couldn't see anything other than the mottled grey and blue sky. Her rapid heartbeat slowed. Perhaps they had lost the hunter. Perhaps the woman preferred to stay in the shadows, away from the crowd of people. Cora tried to relax.

'C'mon,' said Ogg.

Keeping their heads low, they continued through the square. They were about to turn down a street next to a shop when the crowd in front of them parted.

Cora bumped into the back of Ogg. He had slid to a sudden stop in the middle of the square. And looking up ahead, Cora could see why.

The crowd had parted to reveal the woman with glowing red hands. Cora's heartbeat quickened as the woman stared at them with a smile. She obviously didn't care about crowds at all. And this time, she wasn't alone.

Next to her Cora recognised the short man who knelt on all fours. He giggled as he bounced up and down.

Then there was the sound of large beating wings

again. And the third syphon hunter landed next to the others. His hair sat in spikes on his head.

That must have been the whoosh, she thought to herself.

'Possession is a dirty trick,' said the woman, her voice croaky and dry. She clicked her tongue disapprovingly. 'Even for a syphon.'

Cora stepped forward. She didn't know what she was going to do. Maybe her unstable magic would be enough to distract the hunters long enough for Ogg, Tick and Tock to escape.

'Cora,' whispered Tock. He pointed to her hands. She looked down and saw that the cracks were fading. She hadn't noticed it until now but the headache that had been with her for days had almost disappeared. The uncomfortable rumbling of the magic inside her had quietened. Even the warlock magic lay still. She stared down happily as she watched her hands slowly colour back to normal. The ice-stone necklace had worked.

Where tiredness once was, Cora felt strength fill her up in its place. The magic inside her felt new and powerful. *No more running*, a voice inside her said. But this time, it wasn't the voice that had been with her since Jade City, the one that sounded like stone. It was her own. She looked up at the syphon hunters and couldn't help the smile that spread across her lips.

Chapter Thirty-Eight

L ight snowfall drifted down from the sky.

Cora glanced around the square. The trolls and magical beings that had once crowded around her were now running in the opposite direction. Some hid in shops and others quickly jostled down side streets carrying their belongings. It wasn't long until Cora, Ogg, Tick and Tock, and the three syphon hunters were the only ones left in the empty square.

In front of her, the female hunter lifted her glowing red hands into the air, and Cora saw the red net that had captured her before swivelling out from behind the hunter. Except this net looked different. It looked like a giant, glowing mouth. It had sharp, red teeth and whipped about behind the hunter, lashing from side to side like an eager animal, ready to be let out of its cage.

'You don't have to do this,' called Cora. She snatched up the warlock magic and it dashed to her hands, crackling, black sparks at her fingertips.

The hunter on all fours bounced up and down, letting out a high-pitched giggle with every springing jump.

'Oh, we know,' called the woman with a shrug. 'But we want to.'

Then the red, glowing net flew at them. It shot towards Cora with a fiery crack!

The warlock magic at her hands, Cora grabbed the nearest thing on the ground and threw it in front of her. It was the box of talking tambourines. 'What fine weather we have. Did you see the score of the big game? Should you be wearing that hat?' the tambourines chattered as the box went soaring into the air before crashing into the mouth of the red glowing net. The net stopped in the air, snaring the tambourines in its grasp and dropping to the ground. The red glowing teeth then crunched down onto the box ferociously, tearing apart the tambourines. The chattering stopped as pieces of tambourine flew into the air amongst the snow.

Cora swallowed. That was also new. She made a mental note not to let the net with teeth get too close to her and her friends.

Quickly, Cora grabbed onto the princess's magic. Calling up the frosty wind, the air swirled faster and faster around her, rapidly picking up snow on

the ground as it whirred loudly, growing bigger and stronger.

Ahead of them, the hunter with wings shot up into the sky like an arrow.

Tick and Tock looked at Cora before nodding and soaring up into the air too. The flying hunter dove at Cora. Tick and Tock expertly flew into the hunter's way as he barrelled through the sky towards them. The fairies sent sparks towards him, one singeing his wing. The hunter faltered and flew away from Cora, Tick and Tock flying after him.

'You'll have to do better than that,' Tick said.

Tock stuck his tongue out at the hunter and sent more sparks of magic in his direction.

'Cora!' called Ogg next to her.

Cora shouldn't have taken her eyes off the hunters on the ground. She looked back to find the net with teeth flying at her again, its mouth opened wide.

Cora threw the wall of wind that she held in her hands towards the net. The wind hit the net, sending the glowing mouth tumbling backwards towards the hunters. It chomped the air madly as it spun out of control. Cora winced as both of the hunters dove out of the way of the flying net easily.

You'll have to do better than that, Cora repeated Tick's words to herself. If they were going to stop the hunters, she needed to do better. She needed to do more.

Cora looked over at Ogg. She wanted to tell him to go. To find somewhere safe. To help get the others to safety, away from the town square and the syphon hunters. But he met her gaze and squared his shoulders, his feet firmly in place.

He wasn't going anywhere.

Cora watched the syphon hunters leap up from the ground and step closer to them in the square. She thought about the magic inside of her. There was a magic that she hadn't tried yet. The magic that had sat sluggishly inside her since they had escaped from the council. The one she had syphoned in darkness.

'You're just a child!' cried the female hunter angrily. 'A dirty syphon child who —' the woman stopped. And Cora could see that she had been hit in the face ... with a very large snowball.

Cora looked at Ogg, who was next to her, smiling from ear to ear, another snowball already in his hands.

Then something soared past Cora's ear. It wasn't a snowball. It was a dart. The jumping hunter ran towards them, giggling and throwing darts in their direction.

Ogg and Cora ducked out of the way of the dangerous darts just in time. They dove behind one of the large rocks that sat in the square.

'What now?' asked Ogg.

Cora glanced up at the fairies and saw them flutter just out of reach of the flying hunter as he angrily tried to grab hold of them.

'I have an idea,' Cora said to Ogg. She hoped it would work.

'What is it?' asked Ogg eagerly.

Darts hit the stone they hid behind, ricocheting off it.

TING! TING! TING!

Cora waited until she couldn't hear any more *TING*s of flying darts.

'The idea … is that you stay here,' said Cora.

'What?' asked Ogg.

Then without explaining, Cora stepped out from behind the rock. And walked into the square towards the syphon hunters.

Chapter Thirty-Nine

Cora stood in the empty square. The cool wind had picked up, and the snow had begun to fall heavier around them. From the other side of the square, the woman with the glowing red hands smiled at her. The jumping man did the same, clapping his hands happily. The syphon hunters wanted her. Not Ogg or Tick or Tock.

'Look who's ready to play,' said the woman.

The jumping hunter giggled again.

Cora stared down the syphon hunters.

The jumping hunter somersaulted in the air, throwing three darts her way, his hands moving rapidly as he flung each dart.

Snatching up the warlock magic, Cora stopped the darts in the air. She turned them around and sent them soaring back the way they had come — towards the jumping hunter. The hunter stopped giggling, dodging each dart that spun towards him. But Cora had known he would. Cora took the princess's magic and using a gust of wind, she pushed it at the jumping hunter while he was in the air, sending him backwards and into the woman with glowing red hands.

They fell into a heap, their faces landing in the snow.

Behind her, a loud squawk tore through the air followed by a *whoosh* from above. Glancing up, Cora saw the winged hunter plummet down from the sky, and this time, he was heading for her.

With her warlock magic, Cora held her hands up and just like she had done with the darts, she stopped the hunter in the air. The flying hunter's face contorted with rage as he kicked and clawed where he was stuck in the air, fighting against her hold. But it was no use. She held onto him, gritting her teeth with effort.

Then Cora pushed the flying syphon hunter, throwing him backwards with her magic, sending him hurtling into a shop nearby. The hunter went crashing through the shop door and into the store, the walls shaking.

Cora heard the net before she saw it. She spun around just in time to see its sharp teeth descend upon her. She threw her hands up and snatching the Jinx magic, she held onto the glowing red mouth, pushing it away from her, just as a dart flew past her ear.

Tick and Tock flew down to her, sending sparks of magic at the jumping hunter. He turned and dove down a street, away from the fairies. Tick and Tock flew after him, still sending sparks at his jumping back as they disappeared down the Troll Town street.

The glowing red teeth were now inches from her face. They tried chomping down, but Cora pushed against them, holding the mouth away from her with her hands.

A flash of something moved nearby. Out of the corner of her eye, Cora saw Ogg leap out from behind the rock and run down the middle of the square, towards the woman with glowing red hands. Cora's heart dropped.

She waited for Tick and Tock to show up, to fly out and protect Ogg, but the fairies weren't anywhere to be seen. The square was empty.

Then out of a street, Cora saw the jumping hunter bounce back into the square. She waited for Tick and Tock to do the same. But they didn't. Her mind filled with images of the fairies somewhere, hurt.

The jumping hunter turned and saw Ogg. But Ogg didn't see him. Ogg bounded towards the woman with glowing red hands.

And then before Cora could do anything, the jumping syphon hunter threw a pair of darts in Ogg's direction.

'Ogg!' Cora cried.

She watched the darts sail through the air, heading straight for the troll. She pushed against the red net in her hands. Ogg was almost at the other end of the square; he was too far away for her to reach him. She had to let go of the Jinx magic that was protecting her from the net. With one hand she let go of the net and grabbed the warlock magic. Using it, she pushed the blanket of snow on the ground in front of Ogg upwards. It shot up, forming a thick white wall of snow in front of him. The darts flew into it harmlessly, the snow wall shielding Ogg.

Without the Jinx magic, Cora was thrown to the ground by the powerful net. She squirmed out of the way of the chomping mouth as best as she could. It dove on top of her and grabbed handfuls of snow either side of her head.

Bright sparks hit the net. It was Tick and Tock. They flew towards her. They were okay. She felt strength in her again.

Cora reached for the Jinx magic and stopped. The magic that had sat sluggishly inside her moved to the forefront. It wanted her to use it. Cora held onto the new magic. Gently at first and then all at once, it filled her up. And then she felt it *lift* her up. Her whole body floated up from the ground. The net still in her hands, Cora flew up into the air.

She … she … she was flying.

Below her, Ogg and the syphon hunters stared up at her. From the air across the square, Tick and Tock stared at her wide-eyed.

Then stopping in the air, Cora grabbed onto the Jinx magic once more and pulled. With a hand on each side of the net, she pulled the mouth open until it ripped apart in her hands. It stopped glowing, and crackled as it fell to the ground in pieces.

Cora stood floating in the air.

Whoa.

It felt like she was a feather afloat in the wind. Her hands by her side, Cora steadied herself, trying not to move too much otherwise she would lose her balance.

There was another squawk and another *whoosh*. And Cora spun around just in time to see the flying hunter, his wrinkled face inches from hers as he dove at her, his winged arms outstretched towards her.

Before she knew what she was doing, Cora grabbed the witch's magic and clicked her fingers. She appeared back on the ground and watched the winged syphon hunter fly headfirst into a shop roof.

Cora had appeared right where she wanted to be. Behind the woman with the glowing red hands.

Sensing her, the hunter whirled around and two glowing red fists flew Cora's way. Cora caught them both in her hands.

'It won't be long until he finds you,' said the woman.

'Who?' asked Cora, holding tightly to the woman's fists.

The woman pushed Cora back and Cora stumbled, her boots sliding in the loose snow.

The female hunter then conjured up another net with her glowing hands. She pulled and shaped it as it rose from her palms like a web. Before she could finish, Cora dove at the woman but the syphon hunter kicked out, pushing Cora onto the snow.

The syphon hunter laughed.

As she lay on her side, Cora thought of her syphon family. *Hunted and killed.* She thought about what Dann had said. About them disappearing. Magical beings like the syphon hunters *destroying* them. She thought about the memory she had. The field, the pointed, red leather shoes. The dress. The laugh.

An anger rippled through Cora. The wind had picked up around her. It blew furiously by her as she glared at the syphon hunter. Grabbing onto the flying magic, she rose up from the ground and dove at the syphon hunter.

Clasping the woman's glowing red hands in hers, Cora held down the Jinx magic. She felt the woman's glowing red hands go limp.

The syphon hunter cried out as her hands stopped glowing red. Then switching to the warlock magic, Cora threw the syphon hunter up into the air.

Suddenly, a dart shot her way. Instinctively, Cora caught it with the warlock magic. The dart hovered in the air next to her, black sparks hovering around it. She didn't need her hands.

With just her mind, Cora pushed the dart at the giggling hunter and it flew at him with speed, sticking into his arm. The hunter stopped jumping. And then with a final giggle, he fell to the ground.

'You can't run forever,' said the woman angrily, her feet kicking in the air pointlessly as she clutched onto her injured hand.

'I don't plan to,' Cora said.

She conjured up the princess's magic and in seconds the wind and snow were a tempest around them. Using her mind, Cora spun the wind. Faster and faster, she moved it around, whirling the wind with her magic. Quickly, she created a vortex, a tornado. It was taller than the shops, growing larger in the centre of the town square.

Nearby, Ogg grabbed onto Tick's and Tock's hands, pulling them away from the wind, and leading them down a side street from the square.

The wind, a roaring tunnel, spun as it grew, moving around the square. Shops shuddered where they stood, some lost their roofs and windows as they were collected into the spinning wind. It picked up the winged syphon hunter who had emerged out of the smashed roof. The hunter spun around in the tornado of wind, unable to fly out of it. The whirlwind then moved closer, picking up the jumping hunter from where he lay on the ground.

'You're — you're just a child!' cried the woman as she realised what was happening behind her. 'With one eye!'

Then using the Jinx magic, Cora gritted her teeth and threw the female syphon hunter into the roaring whirlwind that spun behind her. The woman crashed into it with a cry, joining the other hunters as they swirled around, trapped inside the roaring vortex. Cora pushed the wind out as hard as she could and it moved up and over Troll Town, spiralling into the air towards the furthest mountain she could see, until the syphon hunters were nothing but a whirring speck in the distance.

Cora fell to her knees in the snow, exhausted.

Chapter Forty

Tick and Tock flew over to Cora on the ground, covering her in a hug with their fairy wings and arms.

'That was amazing,' said Tock.

'That was better than amazing,' said Tick. 'That was atrocious!'

'Astounding,' corrected Tock.

'Astounding!' cried Tick.

Ogg ran over to the three of them. 'I … I …' he said, his eyes wide with excitement. 'Wow!'

When the fairies let go of her, Cora stood up from the ground. She glanced down at her hands. The black cracks were entirely gone. Her fingers, hands and arms were back to normal. She turned both of her hands over and wiggled her fingers. They were hers again. Relief and happiness bubbled inside her like troll stew.

Cora glanced in the distance. The whirling wind of syphon hunters was no longer in sight. She turned and smiled at Tick and Tock. 'We did it.'

'You did it,' said Tock.

'We just helped,' added Tick.

Cora felt good to finally have control of all the magic that sat inside her. And, she had discovered what the magic was that she had syphoned from the council. *But whose was it?*

'I … I think I can fly,' she said to the fairies.

'Levitate,' said Tock.

'No wings,' said Tick, motioning to his own.

'Is it … did I …' Cora began.

'Syphon magic from a vampire?' finished Tock.

'Yes,' said Tick.

Cora froze. She had really, really hoped it was *anyone* but the vampire's magic.

'Am I going to …' she paused, horrified. 'Turn into a bat … or drink … blood?'

Tick laughed.

Tock shook his head. 'You can't syphon all a magical being's power, remember?'

Cora relaxed, thankful that she only syphoned the vampire's levitation power.

'Sircane is the oldest vampire in the whole kingdom,' said Tick.

'Will he be happy?' asked Tock.

'No,' said Tick, shaking his head.

Cora winced.

'Are vampires ever happy?' asked Tock.

'No,' said Tick, shaking his head again. The fairy put his hand to his mouth in a whisper, 'Not enough sunlight.'

'Sircane Montague?' asked Ogg. 'The vampire on the council?' He turned to Cora. 'You syphoned *his* magic?'

Cora nodded.

Ogg's eyes were wide as he stared at Cora. 'That's why they are looking for you?'

Tick and Tock nodded.

Cora noticed that the ground was splintered down the middle. Like an earthquake had ripped through Troll Town.

'Did you see that snowball I threw?' asked Ogg, his eyes shining.

Cora smiled.

'And when the hunter flew into the shop?' added Ogg.

The fairies laughed.

Behind Ogg, a small troll appeared in a flurry of snow. Cora recognised her as the same troll who had spoken to Ogg on their way to Dann's shop. The one with a cane in her hand and long, grey hair tied in many small plaits.

The Troll Queen.

'The way you both chased the hunter down the side street,' Ogg continued. His back was to the Troll Queen and he was too busy recounting what had happened moments ago to realise someone stood behind him.

Then Tick and Tock noticed the Troll Queen, too, the smiles on their faces falling.

'And how Cora created that whirlwind. And did you see …' Ogg stopped, noticing Cora and the fairies' faces. 'What is it?'

Tick and Tock pointed behind the troll.

Ogg turned around and jumped slightly when he saw the Troll Queen. 'Oh.'

The Troll Queen stared up at the four of them, her face creased with tiny lines. In a way, she reminded Cora of Dot. But where Cora knew Dot would be angry, the Troll Queen appeared calm. She rested two hands on her cane as she looked pointedly at Ogg.

'Prince Oggmund the Third,' she began, 'what am I going to do with you?'

Tick and Tock stared wide-eyed at Cora. Cora couldn't help but do the same back at them.

'*Prince?*' she gasped. *Ogg the half troll was a prince?*

Ogg glanced at the three of them, running a hand through his hair uncomfortably.

Tick and Tock bowed in the air towards the queen. In her haste, Cora did a clumsy sort of half-bow half-curtsy.

'Your friends have made a bit of a mess,' said the Troll Queen, glancing around her.

Looking around the square properly, Cora saw the damage she, Tick and Tock had wrought. Some of the roofs on the shops and houses that sat in the square were completely blown off. Others were hanging by a thread. Some windows were shattered.

Cora swallowed.

'But Mother, the syphon hunters —' Ogg spluttered.

The Troll Queen closed her eyes and shook her head, not wanting to hear his explanation.

'It wasn't his fault, Your Majesty,' said Cora, stepping forward. 'It was mine. I did this.'

The Troll Queen glanced up at her.

'I'm sorry. Ogg was just trying to help,' said Cora.

Tick and Tock nodded, flying next to her.

'And we made him bring us here,' said Tock.

That isn't entirely true, thought Cora.

'And we forced him to give us delicious dew suckles,' added Tick.

Definitely not even a little bit true.

The queen stared at the three of them. Her mouth formed a thin line as she tapped a finger on the top of her cane in thought.

'Hunters in Troll Town. Fairies in Troll Town,' said the queen. 'And soon the council will be in Troll Town.'

Cora glanced at Tick and Tock. *Soon?*

'You should leave before they arrive,' the Troll Queen said politely, noticing Cora's glance.

'What about ...' Tock gestured to the mess of the town square.

'This isn't that bad,' said the queen with a shrug. 'You should see the town after Trolltide. I found a shop upside down once.'

The queen smiled at them and Cora was relieved to see that she wasn't angry about the destruction that they had caused. Something else twinkled in the queen's eyes as she looked at her.

'We are leaving now,' said Ogg, taking a step to move past the queen.

'Oggmund.'

Suddenly, the troll was pushed backwards to where he stood. Ogg tried to take another step, but a magic held him in place. They watched as he pushed against it, frustration creasing his face.

'Your *friends*,' repeated the Troll Queen. 'Not you.'

'But —'

The Troll Queen shook her head.

Ogg stopped fighting the magical hold. 'What about my big adventure?' he asked.

'I think you have had enough adventure for a little while,' said the queen.

Ogg kicked the snow at his feet.

Cora felt guilty. If it wasn't for them, Ogg would

still be on his adventure, drawing all the magical creatures he could find.

'Besides, it's not every day a troll prince throws a snowball at a syphon hunter,' added the Troll Queen with a smile.

Ogg's face lit up at her words.

Then in a *POP!* of magic, a fairy suddenly appeared in the Troll Town square.

'Not another one,' said the Troll Queen.

'Fizz?' greeted Tock, wide-eyed.

It was Fizz, one of King Clang's fairy guards.

The fairy flew over to them.

'Tick,' said Fizz.

'Fizz,' said Tick.

'Tock,' said Fizz.

'Fizz,' said Tock.

'Cora,' said Fizz.

'Fizz,' said Cora. 'Is everything alright? How did you find us?'

'I have an urgent message from King Clang,' said Fizz. 'The council know where you are. They are on their way. You must leave. Now. Before they arrive.'

The fairies nodded.

'Is Father okay?' Tick asked.

Fizz nodded. 'They are watching him. Closely.'

The fairies whirled around to Cora.

'Time to go,' said Tock.

'Wait,' said Cora.

'If the council are on their way, then they will be here in seconds,' said Tick.

'Let them come,' said Cora.

'What?' asked Tick, Tock, Fizz, Ogg and the Troll Queen all at the same time. Five pairs of surprised eyes landed on her.

'I don't want to run anymore,' she said. It was true. She didn't want to keep running. Ever since she had left Urt, it felt like that was all she had done.

'Cora,' said Tick, pausing. 'That's quite possibly the worst idea you've ever had.'

'I agree,' said Fizz.

'Tick! Fizz!' said Tock. Then turning to Cora, 'Perhaps don't think of it as running,' continued the fairy. 'Think of it more like we are simply leaving quickly in another direction?'

'This is the council we are talking about,' said Tick. 'We are lucky to have escaped them at all.'

There was a silence. A sea of thoughts swirled in Cora's mind. She thought of her syphon family. She still wanted to find them. But what if Dann was right? What if the syphons didn't want to be found? What if they had been hiding this whole time? Then that meant she would lead the council right to them. The only option was to stay and fight the council. She had fought syphon hunters and won, after all. Could she not do it again?

'Listen to the fairies, dear,' said the Troll Queen. 'For once, they might be right.'

Tick and Tock opened their mouths to say something but then decided against it.

The Troll Queen stepped forward towards her, pressing down on her cane.

'I saw what you did here,' she said. 'I saw you protect my son.'

Then Cora finally understood the look in the queen's eyes. The old troll's pair of bright blue eyes shone with gratitude.

'You can't hide what you are,' the Troll Queen said. 'And I have been in this world long enough to know that some things are worth fighting for.'

Cora nodded.

'But only,' said the queen, 'at the right time.'

Cora paused. She let the Troll Queen's words sink in. Perhaps now, in the middle of the ramshackled Troll Town square, just after narrowly escaping a group of syphon hunters, wasn't the right time to take on the rulers of the magical world.

The Troll Queen placed a hand on Cora's. 'You can't do it alone.'

As Cora stared into the Troll Queen's eyes, she realised that she was right. She remembered what had happened when the council had captured them before. If the council were coming for her, she needed a plan. She needed to be prepared. And she needed help. They needed to leave Troll Town and find her syphon family. Even if she was leading the council straight to them, she needed to know the truth. Why hadn't they taken her with them?

Slowly, Cora nodded to the Troll Queen.

Tick and Tock broke into smiles.

'Good luck,' said Fizz, nodding to the fairies. And with a *POP!* of magic, the fairy guard disappeared.

'Thank you for your horoscope,' said Tick to the Troll Queen.

'Hospitality,' corrected Tock. 'It has been a delight.'

Ogg turned to them. He pulled his notebook from his pocket. He tore out a page from the back of it and handed it to Cora. It was a map of the northern towns. 'We won't say anything,' he said, standing tall. 'When the council come.'

'Thank you,' Cora said. She paused before enveloping Ogg in a hug.

Tick and Tock did the same.

'You know, Troll Town's not so bad,' said Tick, letting go of him.

Ogg laughed. 'Maybe sometime I can visit The Hollow?'

Tick and Tock stopped. 'We wouldn't go that far.'

The fairies flew next to Cora.

'Where to?' Tock asked.

Cora didn't need to think for much longer than a second. 'Tynth,' she said, remembering the place Ogg had said. Then with a final wave to Ogg and the Troll Queen, Tick, Tock and Cora disappeared with a *POP!* of magic.

Chapter Forty-One

In that *POP!* of magic, Cora and the fairies landed in front of a row of tall, narrow houses.

'Is this Tynth?' Cora asked. She took out the map that Ogg had given her.

'I can't see any mud pits and,' said Tick as he breathed in with a snort. 'I can breathe perfectly.'

'Without a memory, fairy travel can be tricky,' said Tock. 'But we should be close.'

On the map, in very tiny writing, she saw the word Tynth squished between Yop and Brug. They were no longer on the outer towns. Instead, they were right near the middle. Right where Gromp the changeling had told them *not* to go.

'We should be in Yop,' said Tock, peering over her shoulder at the map.

The three of them walked towards the houses and shops. They stretched up, four slanting storeys high, and sat in neat rows side by side. On the other side of the buildings was a small circle made of grass. It was soft and springy beneath Cora's feet.

Yop wasn't as colourful or busy like Brolg. Each building in the town was coloured in brown and black. Even the magical beings that walked past them wore brown and black clothes, blending into the town.

Cora and the fairies walked past a shop that sold tap-dancing ties. The brown and black ties clicked and clacked on a table by the shop door. Cora thought that Wilfred, the man who sold hugs in Urt and was a guardian of the gateway, would have loved a tap-dancing tie. Next to the table of ties was a store that sold black and brown flying wigs. The locks of hair flapped in the store window like wings.

In the middle of the town circle, a magical being sat reading a book. A few others stood around him, listening.

As they stepped into the town circle, Cora felt many pairs of eyes watching her. Glancing around, Cora noticed the creatures that were in the town were all staring at her and the fairies.

Cora saw a group of winged magical beings quickly glance away. She saw three women in black robes, hunched over and whispering to one another, their eyes flicking over to her. And as they walked past the magical being in the middle of the circle, he stopped reading his book and closed it. And a man with hairy, green legs actually stopped abruptly on seeing them. Then he turned and walked in the opposite direction.

'Um, Cora,' came Tick's voice.

Cora turned and saw what Tick and Tock were staring at. She stopped walking. Bolted to large rocks scattered throughout the town circle, were gold sheets. In every window, on every wall in front of them, were shimmering gold posters. Cora and the fairies walked over to the nearest glinting one.

Moving across the gold sheets were images of Cora, Tick and Tock. In the image, Cora stood glaring with her red hair and missing eye. She looked mean. And in Tick's and Tock's images, the fairies snarled, their wings sharply beating behind them. Words in a language she couldn't read were written across the top. And a round, red seal was burnt into the gold sheet.

'An Order of Removal,' whispered Tock, his eyes wide.

'Removal?' echoed Cora.

'From the magical world,' said Tick, a waver in his voice.

Cora swallowed. 'That doesn't sound good.'

'It's not,' said Tick. 'It's bad.'

'Very bad,' said Tock.

'What does it mean?' Cora asked, trying not to think about all the ways in which they could be *removed*.

'It means that there is a reward for our capture,' said Tock.

'And we would have to live in the human world,' said Tick, swallowing. 'With … *humans*.'

'Father would never allow it,' said Tock, shaking his head.

'He must have been outvoted,' said Tick.

'But …' said Tock, unbelieving.

The fairies were silent as they stared at the gold sheets in front of them. Cora could see pools of fear and sadness colour the fairies' eyes. Once again they were to be banished, and this time not only from their home, but their entire world. And once again, it was her fault. She could only guess at what the posters said. *Dangerous girl. One eye. Out of control magic.* And it was true. Her powers had been dangerous and her magic had been out of control. But Tick and Tock didn't deserve to be removed from their world.

Cora grabbed Tock's hand and gave it a squeeze. 'I won't let them remove you,' she said. And she meant it.

Tock gave Cora a small smile. Then as if shaken by her words, the fairies straightened.

'Does it say that I am a syphon?' Cora asked.

The fairies shook their heads.

'I think the Orders of Removal are supposed to scare us,' Tock said.

Tick nodded. 'They must want everyone to know who we are.'

'So that we can't hide,' said Cora, realising. She thought about her family. If they had been hiding successfully for years, then maybe they could stay with them? Hidden away from the council? The Orders of Removal explained why everyone in Yop was looking at them like they knew them. They did know them. How long had the posters glinted around the town? And how many other towns were they in?

'We need to find the other syphons,' said Cora. 'Quickly. Before we're recognised.'

'That's it,' said Tick suddenly.

There was a *POP!* of magic and something warm and itchy fell on her head.

'Ta-da! Disguises!' said Tick.

Cora turned to find the hairy fairy had become even more hairy. Sitting on top of Tick's head was one of the very fashionable flying wigs they had seen in the Yop store window.

The fairy twirled, showing off his new long black hair.

Tock was wearing a wig too. He flew to the ground, and flicked his new short brown hair over his shoulders.

Tick looked at Tock and burst into a fit of giggles. Then Tock did the same as he stared at Tick. Cora smiled at the sight of both fairies in fashionable wigs. Cora didn't need to guess that she must be wearing a flying wig too. It was surprisingly heavy on her head and smelt vaguely of dust. She wasn't sure they were going to be enough to disguise them from the magical beings in Yop, but they were better than nothing.

Looking down at the map in her hands, Cora tried to figure out which way would lead them to Tynth the quickest. The less time they spent in Yop, the better. According to Ogg's roughly drawn map, if they continued straight through Yop, they should be in Tynth in a matter of minutes.

Their wigs firmly in place, the three of them kept their heads down as they walked through the remainder of the town circle. Ducking into a few streets, Cora, Tick and Tock wove their way through the small town of Yop. When they reached the end of the town, Cora was relieved to no longer feel the eyes of strangers on her.

They stepped out of the town and noticed that where the town of Yop stopped, so did the lush, green meadow that ran through it. Out in front of them, the ground was dry and cracked. They walked along a short crumbling road and almost immediately came to a sign that stuck out of the rocky ground. Written on the sign were the words: *Welcome to Brug*.

'Brug?!' exclaimed Tock.

Cora stared at the sign, confused. They couldn't have arrived in Brug already. They had only just left Yop. She glanced down at the map. Tynth sat between Yop and Brug. How had they already arrived in Brug?

'That's strange,' Cora said. She glanced behind her. Across the dry road, the brown, narrow buildings and houses of Yop stared back.

'Maybe you're reading it upside down?' suggested Tick.

'Do you have your glasses on?' added Tock.

'I don't wear glasses,' said Cora distractedly.

There was nothing sitting between Yop and Brug. But there should have been a town. They should be standing in Tynth. Maybe Ogg's map wasn't correct?

'Are you lost?' someone asked.

Chapter Forty-Two

Cora, Tick and Tock whirled around to find three creatures standing in front of them, near the *Welcome to Brug* sign.

The being in the middle was a tall and slightly hunched-over man. He reminded Cora of a drooping sunflower. He wore suspenders holding up his trousers, was bald and carried a wooden walking stick though it didn't seem like he needed it. His eyes shifted fervently from Cora to the fairies. Next to him stood two small magical beings. At first Cora thought they were children because they were the same size as Tick and Tock. But by the scowling looks on their wrinkling faces, Cora realised that the pair weren't children at all. They were old men. Very small and very angry, old men. One of the old men had green hair and the other one had blue.

Syphon hunters? Cora wondered. She couldn't tell.

The three magical beings stepped away from the sign and walked towards them along the rocky road.

Cora steadied herself as they approached.

'You three are famous, you know,' said the man with the hunched back.

Cora wasn't sure she liked the sound of that.

'We don't know what you're talking about,' said Tick. 'We are just nobodies who are passing through.' He flicked his wig casually over his shoulders.

'Oh,' said the man. 'Is that so?'

Tock nodded, tossing his hair too. 'We are just on our way to Tynth.'

The man's thin eyebrows rose.

Cora wasn't sure that Tock should have mentioned Tynth. But it was too late.

'Tynth?' echoed the man.

The two old men laughed either side of him.

'Are you sure you want to go to Tynth?' asked the man.

'Stay here. It's much better than Tynth,' said the old man with green hair. 'We have grass. And sky. We have that shrub over there.'

Cora looked at the shrub that sat near the *Welcome to Brug* sign. It looked like a regular shrub.

'Tynth probably doesn't have a shrub like that,' said the old man with blue hair.

'Or a nice rock like that one,' said the green-haired magical being pointing to a small rock by Cora's feet.

'Do you know what lies in Tynth?' asked the hunched magical being. 'You wouldn't last a second.'

'The gas will get you,' said the old man with green hair.

'Or you will get trapped in a mud pit,' said the other old man.

'We'll take our chances,' said Cora.

The man in the middle paused. 'You don't know where it is, do you?'

Cora glanced at Tick and Tock.

The man laughed again. 'They don't know where it is,' he said to the colourful old people.

There was something about the magical beings that was unsettling. Why were they asking them all of these questions? Why did they care if they went to Tynth? Why were they here?

'What do you want?' Cora asked.

'Oh, where are my manners?' replied the tall man, stepping forward. 'My name is Tuff. And this is Rash and Dash.' He pointed to the old men next to him. They waved wrinkled fingers at them.

Cora wasn't sure what kind of magical beings they were but she noticed that both Rash's and Dash's eyes were an unusual red colour. And that it didn't seem like either of them were particularly fond of blinking.

'And you are?' asked Tuff, motioning to Cora.

Cora, Tick and Tock paused. They hadn't thought of anything past the wig disguises.

Tuff let out another loud laugh that stretched up from his belly. The two old men next to him smirked.

'Those wigs are not going to fool anyone,' said Tuff, pretending to wipe a tear away from his eye. Then the man set his eyes on Cora. 'You're the girl with the missing eye,' he said, pointing a finger with a sharp, bruised nail on it in her direction. 'The council is offering a lot of gold for you.'

And there it was. They weren't syphon hunters at all. They were just greedy.

'Along with fairy one and fairy two,' said Tuff pointing at the fairies.

'It's Tick,' said Tock, folding his arms.

'And Tock,' said Tick, also folding his arms.

Tuff smiled.

Cora stepped to the side, hoping to walk around the group. But Rash stepped to the side too, blocking her path.

'Let us pass,' said Cora.

But the three strangers stood still.

'You're not going to Tynth,' said the man. 'You're not going anywhere.'

'Other than with us, of course,' said the two old men together.

Chapter Forty-Three

Cora squared her shoulders at the magical beings in front of them. She glanced at Tick and Tock. Then, determinedly, Cora straightened the wig on her head. Tick and Tock did the same with theirs.

But before Cora could even think to use her magic, the man called Tuff gave a sharp whistle. And Rash and Dash leapt forward, lunging at Tick and Tock. The fairies jumped back, flying up into the air but the pair of old men were surprisingly quick and grabbed onto the fairies' feet before they could get very far.

'Let them go,' Cora said. She flung her warlock magic to her fingers.

'Ooh, dark magic,' said Tuff, an impressed tone in his voice. 'No wonder the council is after you.'

Tick and Tock struggled against the hold of Rash and Dash. They threw sparks of magic at the pair but they twisted and turned out of harm's way.

Then Rash and Dash shimmered in the air. And their coloured hair morphed into black and brown flying wigs. Their wrinkled old faces softened. They sprouted fairy wings and big bellies. They had become Tick and Tock. Their clothes, their eyes, their cheeky expressions. They were exactly the same.

Cora stared wide-eyed at the four fairies that tussled with each other in the air. She was so distracted, she didn't see Tuff lunge at her until it was too late. She spun around and a large black sack was almost over her head. Holding the witch's magic, she snapped her fingers and appeared behind Tuff.

The man whirled around. But Cora already had the warlock magic in her hands. She held her hand out and snatched the sack from Tuff then threw it over the hunched magical being. He tripped over, falling to the ground in the sack.

Cora looked up at the fairies. Two Ticks and two Tocks fluttered in the air sending sparks of magic at one another. Cora realised that she didn't know which was the real Tick and which was the real Tock.

'Cora, it's us,' said one Tock.

'No, it's us,' said another Tock.

Cora stopped, her magic in her hand. The four fairies flew in front of her, twisting and turning and diving in the air. She couldn't tell them apart. She didn't know where to throw her magic.

'Cora, look out!' said Tick.

'Cora, look out!' said the other Tick.

The sack that covered Tuff on the ground suddenly ignited in flames. The sack fell apart, pieces of it burning to ash. And Cora watched as the magical being stood up, brushing burning fragments from his clothes.

This was going to be harder than she'd thought.

'Tell me where Tynth is,' said Cora, holding an arm out.

The man laughed.

Cora thought that would be his response.

'Even if I told you,' said the man. 'You need a key to get there. Which I am pretty sure you don't have.'

Cora saw a small brass key hanging from the man's waist. She clicked her fingers, appeared next to him, snatched the key, and then clicked her fingers again before the man even knew what had happened.

Cora held the key in her hand and stared back defiantly at Tuff. He searched his waist and Cora thought he was going to growl angrily at her as his hands brushed against nothing. Instead, the man smiled when he realised what she had taken and then let out another loud, belly-shaking laugh.

'Not that kind of key,' he said.

Crud.

Cora searched the rocky road around them for anything that looked remotely like it could be used as a key. *But what kind of key?* A key could be anything. She looked at the shrub. She looked at the rocks.

'That key is for my house,' said Tuff, pointing at the key in her hand. 'I'm going to need it back.'

Then Cora felt like she was being pushed along the rocky road by an invisible hand. Tuff was pulling her towards himself. She dug her heels into the ground.

Tuff laughed and Cora was well and truly tired of the sound.

Then calling up the wind she held it up in front of her. The wind blew, hitting the magical being forcefully. He stumbled and his hold fell from her.

'His stuff,' called one of the Ticks amongst the jostling Ticks and Tocks.

'Staff,' corrected Tock.

Cora looked at Tuff. The wooden cane he held in his hand glinted slightly in the light. It wasn't a walking stick like she had thought.

Not only that, Cora knew straight away which of the fairies were the real Tick and Tock and which weren't. Warlock magic at her fingers, she grabbed onto the staff with her magic. Tuff's eyes went wide as he felt her hold. He pushed hard against her with the invisible hand. And Cora flew backwards.

But her hold stayed on the staff. From the ground Cora made a fist with her hands and watched as the staff in Tuff's hands splintered in two.

Tuff growled in anger, his round dark eyes filled with hatred.

Standing up, Cora used her warlock magic to grab onto the Tick and Tock impostors and threw them as hard as she could, right into Tuff.

The fake fairies shot backwards in the air, colliding into Tuff with a bang.

The three magical beings fell to the ground in a heap. Cora walked over and watched as the two fairies shimmered back into old men with coloured hair. The three of them slumped together, knocked out.

Cora dropped the key she held to the ground, next to the magical beings.

Tick and Tock flew down to her.

'Phew,' said Tick. 'Good thing you know us so well.'

Tock kicked the foot of one of the old men. They didn't stir.

'What are they?' Cora asked.

'Shapeshifters,' said Tock.

'And a demon,' said Tick.

A demon? Cora looked down at Tuff and the key that sat on the ground. Was he telling the truth about Tynth and needing a key?

The soft sound of a person clapping filled the air around them.

Spinning around, the fairies wasted no time in bowing in response to the clapping. 'Thank you,' said Tick. 'Thank you.'

'We couldn't have done it without you,' said Tock, graciously.

Then the fairies looked up from their bows to see who it was that was clapping for them.

'Cora,' said Tock.

The clapping stopped.

'What's in Tynth?' asked a voice behind her.

Cora was about to whirl around with her magic in her hands. But the familiarity of the voice made her stop in her tracks. She waited, unsure if she was hearing things. Her magic was fixed. She shouldn't be hearing voices. And this voice was a voice she hadn't known she would ever hear again. A voice that had been with her ever since she could remember.

'Don't tell me you've forgotten me already,' said the voice again.

And Cora knew exactly who it belonged to. Her heart leapt inside her chest and she spun around to face the owner.

Cora almost collapsed where she stood.

There, standing with a pack on her back, a cat in her arms, and a smile on her warm face was … Dot.

Chapter Forty-Four

Tears sprung to Cora's eyes. Her feet flew as she raced across the rocky ground. She couldn't help the tightness of the hug she flung onto the old woman. Or the smile that lit up her face.

Dot hugged her back just as fiercely. Cora held on, not wanting to let go.

From Dot's arms, Scratch placed a rough lick across Cora's face. She laughed. The cat's tongue felt like sand on her skin, just like she remembered.

Cora stared up at Dot. *How did she find me?*

'How …' she tried.

'I escaped with Scratch,' said Dot. 'I only had enough time to play the lullaby, hoping if you went back to the house before I could find you that you would run.'

'I had to go,' said Cora trying to explain why she left Urt. 'The Jinx, it was …'

Dot nodded. 'I know,' she said. 'Wilfred told me.'

Cora was relieved. A happiness filled her just having Dot near.

Cora felt Tick and Tock, fluttering politely a short distance behind her.

Cora let go of Dot. 'And these are my friends,' she said. 'Tick and Tock.'

The fairies flew over to them.

'You're Cora's Dot,' said Tick.

Dot laughed, nodding.

'Tick,' said Tick with a short bow.

'Tock,' said Tock with a short bow.

'They saved me from the Jinx in Urt,' said Cora.

Dot smiled at the fairies. 'It seems I have a lot to thank you for,' she said.

Tick and Tock smiled shyly at the old woman.

Dot glanced at the magical beings behind the fairies. 'And them?'

Cora wasn't quite sure where to begin.

'Ah, a lot has happened since Urt,' said Cora, unsure of where to begin.

'Cora's a syphon,' Tick blurted out. 'She can absorb magic!'

'Tick!' said Tock, elbowing the fairy.

Cora winced.

Then peeking through her eye, she looked up at Dot.

And to her surprise, the old woman smiled down at her.

'And you've changed your hair,' said Dot, touching her wig.

Cora smiled and adjusted her wig. 'How did you find us?' she asked. Had Dot been looking for her this entire time?

'Wilfred said that if I was to have any luck in finding you, that I should try the fairy kingdom,' explained Dot.

Cora couldn't help but be surprised. Dot knew about the fairy kingdom? And the magical world?

'I went there and a nice fairy named Fazz or Fozz told me you had left for the northern towns,' said Dot.

'A fairy named Fizz?' asked Tock.

Dot nodded. 'That's him.'

'I am going to call him Fozz from now on,' said Tick with a giggle.

'We came to the northern towns to look for my ...' Cora paused. Dot and Scratch looked down at her. It suddenly felt strange calling the syphons, whom she had never met, her family. Dot and Scratch were her family. 'We are looking for other syphons in Tynth. But Tynth is —'

'Uninhabitable,' said Tock.

'Filled with mud pits that suck you down into the ground where you can't get out,' said Tick.

'And poisonous gas that clogs the air so that most creatures can't breathe,' said Tock.

'Do you want to come with us?' Cora asked. She didn't want Dot to leave. Not yet. Not ever.

Cora was sure the old woman would say no, or forbid Cora from going to such a dangerous place. But to her surprise, Dot set her mouth in a determined line.

'I wouldn't miss it for the world,' Dot said.

Cora smiled. For the first time in a long time, her heart was full.

'We should hurry,' said Tock.

'Those three bingos might wake up soon,' said Tick, pointing over his shoulder at the pile of magical beings.

'Bozos,' corrected Tock.

Tick was right. They needed to hurry, before the shapeshifters and the demon woke up. But they still didn't know where Tynth was. It was supposed to be right where they were standing. And they still didn't have a key.

'Which way?' Dot asked.

'We don't exactly know,' said Tock.

'The map says it should be here,' said Cora. She showed Dot Ogg's map. The four of them looked around them along the rocky road.

'And Tuff the demon said we needed a key,' Cora said.

'What kind of key?' Dot asked. 'A key could be anything.'

Cora smiled at Dot. She had thought the exact same thing. Cora tried to think of what the key could be. Maybe if they had it, Tynth would reveal itself to them?

'Maybe it's a word,' said Tock. The fairy then

turned to the space in front of them. 'Open up!' he yelled at no one in particular. Nothing happened. 'Nope,' he said.

'Maybe it's a dance,' said Tick. He flew to the ground and danced a complicated series of steps along the ground. Finishing with a flourish and a click, Tick paused and waited. Nothing happened. 'Nope.'

The afternoon sun was hot and the wig on Cora's head was making her hotter. Many minutes passed and they still didn't have an answer. They were still no closer to finding Tynth. Cora grabbed the wig from her head and dropped it to the ground.

It has to be here. There has to be something we're missing. Cora closed her eye and concentrated. She blocked out the noise around her, the sun on her skin.

Then there was a small tug. Cora's eye flew open. The feeling was so light, she almost missed it. But it was there. She paused. Waiting for it to happen again. A tickling sensation tugged at her again. She took a step forward and waited. The tickle returned but softer. She turned and followed the feeling, walking a few steps ahead and then to the left, she let the feeling guide her across the rocky road. She felt another tickle when she turned to the right. And then another with each step she took.

'Cora?' queried Tick.

'Are you making up your own dance?' asked Tock.

'You need to use your elbows more,' said Tick, waving his elbows around.

Cora focused on the tickling feeling. Moving her feet this way and that she walked around the rocky road until the tickling became constant.

When it didn't disappear, Cora stopped. She looked down at her feet. Something pulled her down towards the ground like an invisible rope was tied from her to the ground. She bent down to her knees and the tickling feeling became stronger.

Cora remembered what Tick and Tock had said in Brolg. About the feeling they felt when others of their kind were near. Theirs felt like a hiccup. Could Cora's be a tickle? Was this what Tick and Tock had meant? And if it was, then that could only mean that … *there were syphons nearby.*

Cora's heart quickened with hope. The tickling connection to her kind fluttering inside her like a butterfly. She brushed her hand along the ground in front of her to see if something was hidden beneath the rocks. Then she remembered the dream that she had. The one where she was back in Urt. Her home. And the cracks that split the ground apart from beneath her feet and the flames that rose up from them.

Then suddenly it made sense to Cora. If Tynth was hidden because syphons lived there … then maybe the only way to find it was to … *be* a syphon. Maybe the key the demon was talking about … was her?

Cora looked down at the ground. Hesitantly, she placed a hand, palm down, onto the rocky ground. She closed her eye and waited for something to happen.

Then Cora felt it. Like a key clicking into place, the ground beneath her hand shifted. And suddenly, the earth below her feet rumbled. A crack appeared beneath Cora's hand. It splintered, quickly growing bigger.

Cora lifted up her hand and took a step back.

Tick, Tock, Dot and Scratch were by her side.

'Looks like you found the key,' said Tick.

The cracks grew bigger, spreading out like a web across the dry ground. The rocky road rumbled and shook.

Cora and Dot steadied themselves.

Suddenly the ground split open wide beneath their feet.

'Uh-oh,' said Cora.

With a cry, Cora and Dot fell down into a hole, plummeting headfirst into the dark space below.

Chapter Forty-Five

Cora and Dot fell down, down, down into the dark hole. Scratch screeched in Dot's arms. Cora was about to grab the vampire magic to hover herself and Dot in the air when she felt two fairy hands clutch hold of her beneath her arms. Tick was doing his best to hold her up, his wings fluttering hard behind him. Opposite them, Cora saw that Tock was doing the same for Dot.

The fairies did their best to hold onto them but the fall through the ground above was from too high up, they were tumbling too fast. The fairies tumbled with them, their wings beating hard to stay upright. The ground below them was swiftly rushing up to meet them.

'This is going to be bumpy!' said Tick.

'Hold on!' said Tock.

The fairies, Dot and Cora landed on a patch of bright, green grass. All four of them rolled together across the ground like a snow giant rolling down a snowy mountain in Troll Town. They rolled and rolled along the soft ground until eventually they came to a stop in a heap of arms, legs, wings and a tail.

'Perfect landing,' said Tick, his face pressed into the grass next to Dot.

Cora waited for Dot to say something. The old woman paused. Then she let out a laugh. The quiet air filled with the old woman's delighted chuckle. Cora hadn't known how much she had missed the sound of Dot's laugh until she heard it.

Cora laughed too as she met Dot's gaze. Scratch sat up on Dot's belly and licked his fur.

Above them, Cora saw a hole in the sky. It was like someone had taken a great big bite out of the blue.

Wait a minute, thought Cora. She sat up suddenly.

A crystal blue sky. Soft, bright green grass. She breathed in the air. Clean, fresh and incredibly pleasant. Tynth was supposed to be the *opposite* of this. *Where were the mud pits? And the poisonous gas?*

Rolling over, Cora felt the lush, green grass in her fingers. It was definitely real. Then, standing up, Cora squinted out into the distance. The green hills continued around them all the way to the horizon. The setting afternoon sun coloured the hills with an amber glow. It was beautiful.

Tick and Tock flew up into the air and gazed out onto Tynth. They held their noses closed with two fingers, expecting to smell poisonous gas. But the breeze blew coolly and calmly across their skin. The fairies let go of their noses.

'H–how?' asked Tick, his eyes wide. 'Where are the mud pits that suck you in until you are swallowed whole?'

'And the poisonous air?' asked Tock. 'That turns everyone inside out with the smallest whiff?'

The Tynth that sat before them was more beautiful than anywhere that Cora had ever seen. Dot stood up and joined the three of them.

'The air isn't poisonous at all … it's delightful,' said Tick. He breathed in a large gulp of air with a snort.

Cora looked at Dot confused. The old woman glanced suspiciously around them.

Cora turned to find a cluster of houses sitting huddled together on the grass. They were small cottages with rounded windows and yellow roofs. *Syphons.* Cora stopped, her heart beating fast. Tynth wasn't uninhabitable at all. It was hidden. And what better way to remain hidden than with rumours of mud pits and poisonous air? Ensuring no other magical beings came looking?

Her mind full of thoughts, Cora walked away from the group, her feet taking her in the direction of the nearest house almost of their own accord.

Her eyes unmoving from the cottage ahead of her, Cora pressed down her dress with the palms of her hands and pushed back the strands of hair that had come loose from her ponytail. She was so close. All that was left was finding out what lay behind the cottage doors ahead.

But as she got closer to the cottage, Cora slowed and slowed until her hopeful steps became heavy with dismay. When she reached the front door, all hope of finding her syphon family had fluttered away from Cora like a snowdrift in Troll Town.

Doors ajar, Cora could see that the cottages were empty. Furniture sat dusty and broken inside. Wood had rotted in parts. A few windows had been broken. Paint on the walls had started to peel. Some of the yellow roofs had even collapsed. The cottages were old and abandoned. Just like the houses in Urt.

Magical beings had lived here once. But it was clear, that nobody lived here anymore. Cora let out a sigh of frustration. Was she ever going to find other syphons?

Glancing down, Cora saw something lying half-covered in the grass by her feet. She bent down and picked it up. In her hand she held a small toy. It was a doll carved out of wood. The doll stared back at Cora, a tiny crack running down its middle.

Cora ran a finger over the line that stretched from one of the doll's eyes down to her stomach. Cora felt like there was a crack running down her middle too.

Tick's and Tock's fluttering of wings grew louder behind her. Cora turned to find the fairies and Dot standing nearby, peering at her worriedly.

'Oh, isn't that sweet,' came a voice from somewhere they couldn't see.

Eyes wide, Tick and Tock spun around.

The air in the meadow behind the fairies and Dot shimmered. Into the meadow stepped a man she didn't think they would ever see again. A man with long black hair that was greying at the temples, and a matching black coat and boots.

Archibald Drake, the warlock who had chased her around the magical kingdom and destroyed her ice-stone bracelet, was back.

Chapter Forty-Six

'You brought your grandmother,' Archibald said with a sneer. 'And worse. A cat.'

Scratch hissed in his direction.

Not wasting a second, Cora found the witch's magic and clicked her fingers. She appeared in front of the fairies and Dot, standing between them and the warlock.

Archibald Drake stared down at her.

'Stolen some more magic, have we?' the warlock spat.

Cora didn't flinch at his words. She could see that the warlock's eyes were shallow with dark rings around them. His white skin was stretched even more tightly over his face than Cora remembered. And he looked to be walking with a heavy limp.

The fairies flew next to Cora.

'Quickly,' whispered Tock. 'Let's go.'

Tick placed his hand on her shoulder to magic her away.

But the same feeling that Cora felt in Troll Town returned. She didn't want to run anymore. She was finally where she was meant to be. Where her family once were. And she wasn't going to be chased away.

'No,' she said to them, shrugging Tick's hand away. 'No more running.' She glared at the warlock. 'Didn't the Jinx throw you over a city?'

The warlock snarled at her.

'That was nothing for a warlock,' said Archibald, holding his head up high. But even as he stood up straight, Cora could see the warlock was injured.

'What are you doing here?' Cora asked. She let her anger seep into her voice.

'I heard Tynth was a wonderful spot for a holiday,' said the warlock. Black sparks flickered from the fingers on the warlock's hand.

Tick and Tock readied themselves next to Cora.

Cora watched a smile flicker behind the warlock's eyes. He was enjoying himself. Uneasiness crept inside her like a spider. Thoughts swam in her mind. Had the warlock been following them this whole time and they didn't know it? How else would he know they would be in Tynth? And how did he get here if the town was hidden?

'I know why you're here,' said the warlock. 'A syphon sighting in the northern towns. That is impossible to miss.'

Cora paused. Is that why he was here? Was he chasing the same rumour they were? Cora still felt the tickling sensation prickle inside her. But it didn't make sense. Why was the tickling sensation still tickling if all that was in Tynth was ... an injured warlock?

Then the warlock said something that made the tiny hairs on the back of Cora's neck stand up straight.

'Did the Troll prince deliver my message correctly?' asked the warlock.

Cora stopped. Ogg? Her heart fell. Her body froze. Ogg ... and the warlock? What did Ogg have to do with ... Then she remembered the picture that Ogg had drawn of Archibald Drake in his notebook.

The warlock laughed an icy snicker.

Was Ogg working with Archibald Drake? Cora looked at Tick and Tock, they stared back, eyes wide. Something most definitely was not right.

'Alright, alright, I'll tell you,' he said. The warlock held his arms out as though he was waiting for a round of applause. 'It was *me*.'

Cora, Tick and Tock glared at the warlock. What was he talking about?

The warlock groaned, frustrated at their vacant stares. His hands dropped to his sides. 'I knew you would need another ice-stone bracelet and eventually head to Troll Town to get one. So I went there first and told many of those poor, disgusting trolls that a syphon was seen in Tynth,' said the warlock.

Cora felt the colour drain from her face as she realised what the warlock was saying. King Clang had told them about the rumour ... but it was Ogg who mentioned Tynth. Or rather ... the warlock.

'W-why?' Cora asked. She felt sick.

'So that you would come here,' said the warlock as though it were obvious. 'Where I would be waiting for you.' He spread his arms out either side of him proudly. 'I knew that not even mud pits and poisonous gas would stop you from seeking out more of your kind.'

'You snake,' said Tock.

'Why, thank you,' said the warlock with a bow.

But Cora felt it. The tickling feeling inside her. Her connection to her kind. It was still there. She turned back and looked at the houses.

The warlock laughed. 'There are no other syphons here, girl. There haven't been for many years.'

Cora felt like she had been punched in the guts. *There were no syphons left.* She had been wrong. They had all been wrong. Her whole journey to find syphons in the northern towns had been for nothing.

'It won't be long,' said Archibald.

'Until what?' replied Cora, anger well and truly in her voice now. She let the warlock magic move to her hands.

Archibald Drake smiled a smile she had seen before. One where the smile didn't quite reach his dark, hooded eyes. The smile that wasn't really a smile at all.

A crack of lightning pierced the sky above them and Cora, Tick and Tock jumped at the sudden sound.

Lightning shattered across the bright blue afternoon sky, and looking up, Cora saw that like in her dreams, the lightning was black.

Cora, Tick and Tock moved back, closer to Dot.

A crack of lightning fell from the sky, hitting the ground in front of them. And standing where the lightning had struck, where Cora thought a scorch mark should be, was instead, a man. A man she had only seen in memories and nightmares. A man with hair that shone silver like the glinting moon.

Chapter Forty-Seven

Hands behind his back, the silver-haired man looked just like he had in the princess's memories. Just like he had in Cora's nightmares. He stood tall against the warlock and wore a silver robe to match his hair. His hair glinted in the sun and his robe billowed on its own behind him. As Cora met his gaze, she could see that the man's eyes were a pure white. And he had small scars on his chin and cheeks.

The silver-haired man ran his unsettling white eyes over Cora's features, coming to a stop on her missing eye. He smiled. And the tickling sensation inside Cora became stronger.

'I've been looking for you,' the silver-haired man said in a deep, clipped voice.

Cora swallowed. She felt the muscles in her body tense up and her magic stretched inside her, ready whenever she was.

'I've been looking for you … for years.'

Cora almost gasped at the silver-haired man's words. The man who had destroyed a city and stolen a princess's life ... had been looking for *her*? *For years?* A slow feeling of dread oozed into Cora.

'It is Cora, isn't it?' he asked, taking a step closer.

And he knows my name. Cora stepped back in response. She felt Dot's hand move to her shoulder and Tick and Tock flutter closer beside her.

'I'm Kaede,' he said. 'Do you remember me?'

Cora stared at the silver-haired man. She thought back to her memories from before she lost her eye. Was she supposed to know him? She shook her head.

'We're related you and I,' he said.

Cora stopped as a coldness crept through her. *Related?!* She and the silver-haired man?! HE was her family? *No. No.* He was lying. He had to be.

'I'm a syphon too,' the silver-haired man said, putting a hand to his chest. He held out his other hand in the air. And a small flame ignited. It danced on his palm before turning into ice.

'We are the same,' he said.

No, no, no. It can't be. But deep down Cora knew. She had felt it as soon as he had arrived. The tickling feeling. The connection to her kind. It wasn't leading her to Tynth. It was leading her to *him*. The silver-haired man.

'We're not the same,' Cora said.

'Well, we've both lived here,' Kaede said as he gazed out at the rolling fields of grass. 'On this very plain. Many years ago. When Tynth was a pathetic syphon sanctuary.'

Cora glared at Kaede.

'We have to stick together,' said Kaede. 'We are nearly the last of our kind.'

'You don't know that,' said Cora, shaking her head.

The silver-haired man tilted his. 'Oh, but I do,' he said. 'I made sure of it.'

Archibald Drake smirked by Kaede's side.

'I destroyed every syphon who didn't want to rise up and rule the magical world with me,' the silver-haired man said. 'Except your parents, who managed to escape. With you.'

His words echoed in the air. *He* had destroyed the

syphons. But where were her parents if they'd escaped? Cora placed a hand where her eye should have been. 'You did this,' she whispered.

The silver-haired man stared back at her with a smile. 'No,' he said. 'Your parents did that.'

Cora stopped. She tried to take in everything the silver-haired man had said. Thoughts swirled around in her head. Thoughts and anger. She glared at the man in front of her. Years of not knowing who she was, or where she came from. It was all because of him. He had attacked her family. Just like he'd attacked the princess and the avians.

'Why?' asked Cora.

Kaede settled his eyes on her. 'They were weak. We should have conquered the magical kingdom; no-one would have been able to stop us. But instead, all they wanted to do was run and hide,' the man paused. 'Just like you.'

'Me?' Cora replied.

'You kept her from me,' the silver-haired man said. And this time, Cora watched the man's glare move to look at someone behind her.

Turning, Cora saw that he was talking to Dot. The old woman squared her shoulders defiantly at the silver-haired man.

'I did what her parents asked of me,' said Dot.

My parents? Dot … Dot knows my parents?

Dot looked down at her, pain and guilt glistening in her eyes. *I'm sorry*, they said.

Cora stepped away from Dot and the fairies. She couldn't take it in. All of it was too much. She shook her head and placed her fingers on her temples.

'Oh dear, she didn't tell you?' queried the silver-haired man. He tutted.

Cora wanted to block everything out. Her magic rolled around inside her. She thought of the memories of Princess Avette. Of what Kaede had done to her and her kingdom. She looked back at the cottages. What he had done to other syphons. To her family. Cora felt her anger consume her as she stared at the silver-haired man.

'Will you join me, Cora?' Kaede asked. 'Together we could do many great things.'

Cora glared at the syphon. 'Never.'

'Very well,' Kaede snarled angrily. 'Time to say goodbye.' He stepped forward, his eyes glinting with delight as he pointed a long finger at her.

Suddenly Cora felt her feet turn ice cold. Looking down, she watched ice stretch up from the ground covering her boots. She couldn't move; the ice kept her stuck to the ground. Before the ice could reach her legs, Cora held onto the witch's magic and clicked her fingers. She appeared next to Dot, without her boots.

The silver-haired man clapped his hands. 'Marvellous! Marvellous! Archibald, you never told me she was this far along in her abilities.'

Tick and Tock sent sparks at the silver-haired man. He deflected them with his hands.

'Go, Dot,' said Cora, she pushed the old woman back in the direction of the cottages.

Dot shook her head. 'I made a promise, Cora.'

'Go!' said Cora, turning to the old woman.

Stubbornness glinted in Dot's eyes as she stared at Cora. Then, after a moment, the old woman reluctantly retreated with Scratch to the safety of the empty cottages.

Black lightning shattered across the sky.

Cora stepped forward, her eyes on the man who had destroyed the others of her kind. The man who wanted to destroy her too. He had been looking for her for years and if she ran now, he would only follow. His words echoed in her mind. *All they wanted to do was run and hide.* But where were they now? Was she the last one left? She wasn't going to run or hide anymore.

Archibald sent his magic at Tock. The fairy was squeezed by invisible hands in the air. Cora turned to her friend and using her own warlock magic, she broke Tock free from his hold.

The warlock glared at her as the fairy fluttered higher into the air.

The silver-haired man clapped again, a laugh escaping his lips.

Tick and Tock sent sparks at the warlock, which he struggled to dodge. One hit him in the shoulder and he gasped.

'They don't understand us, you know,' said Kaede, walking casually across the grass. 'None of them do.'

The syphon stopped walking and looked pointedly at her. 'Are you sure you want to do this?'

Cora glared at the man. She hadn't been more sure of anything. She called up the wind around her. It whipped past her ears in a howl as it grew stronger.

A viciousness glinted behind Kaede's white eyes. 'Very well,' he said. 'I wonder if … your brother is just as foolish.'

Chapter Forty-Eight

*B*rother?

With just one word, Kaede had turned Cora's world upside down. *I have a … brother?*

Kaede smirked a deathly smile. 'Oh, you didn't know?'

It was just a distraction. It had to be. Cora shook the thoughts away and gritted her teeth as magic flew to her hands. A powerful wind already in her fist, Cora threw it at the syphon and it barrelled into the silver-haired man like a bullet. Kaede went flying backwards into the air, tumbling down onto the ground with a thump.

Kaede stood up slowly, a smile still on his face. He brushed grass from his silver robe.

'Avian magic. Is that where it went?' he asked. 'I should have destroyed that disgusting bird when I had the chance.'

Then the ground beneath Cora was pushed

upwards, a mound of earth erupting from below her feet sent her shooting up into the sky.

'Ahh!' she cried out. Quickly, Cora grabbed hold of the vampire magic and hovered in the air, steadying herself with the magic.

'Impressive,' said Kaede.

Cora felt invisible hands push her arms flat against her sides. She fought against them but the hold was tight. The invisible hands threw her down towards the ground, fast. Cora tried to get her hands free to use the witch's magic but they were immovable from her sides. She hit the ground, landing on one of her shoulders with a gasp. Pain shot down her arm.

'But not impressive enough,' Kaede finished.

Glancing over, she saw Tick and Tock trapped by Archibald. Conjuring up the warlock magic, she pushed the warlock backwards, giving Tick and Tock enough time to scramble away from his hold.

Then, clicking her fingers, Cora appeared directly in front of Kaede. The syphon took a swipe at her but she clicked her fingers again and appeared behind him. Holding the Jinx magic, she hurled the syphon as hard as she could and he flew ahead of her, skidding across the ground, dirt and grass flying up either side of him.

Kaede groaned angrily.

She called up the princess's magic and threw it at the warlock. He struggled against it. Then cuts appeared in Cora's arms. She pushed him backwards and he flew through the air. Tick and Tock chased after him.

She turned back to the silver-haired man to find him gone. The syphon had disappeared. She spun around on the spot, her heart racing. Then something hard knocked her to the ground.

'You're not the only one with surprises,' came Kaede's voice. Then the silver-haired man appeared out of thin air in front of Cora. He bent down and grabbed her by her injured shoulder before Cora could reach for her magic.

She cried out in pain.

There was a screech and Cora saw something black dive in front of her, hooking its claws into the syphon. It was Scratch. Which meant ...

Turning, she saw Dot with a slingshot in her hand, sending anything and everything she could get her hands on at the syphon. Cora remembered when Dot had found a slingshot in Urt. She had always kept it with her, in case they ever ran into trouble.

The silver-haired man snarled. And lightning crackled across the sky. He threw Scratch from his neck as Cora jumped up. Grabbing onto the Jinx magic she held onto the syphon's silver robe and threw him up into the air as hard as she could, gritting her teeth against the pain in her shoulder.

Tick and Tock sent sparks at the syphon, hitting him in the back as he soared through the air. He hit the ground hard, his silver robe smoking from fairy magic marks.

Cora breathed in and out, waiting. She glanced behind her. The warlock was on the ground, shielding his face from a barrage of rocks flung at him by Dot.

Slowly, Kaede placed two hands on the ground either side of himself. The earth beneath Cora's feet rumbled, but not like it had done before. The entire land of Tynth shook beneath them. Then cracks appeared in the ground like an earthquake. Looking up, Cora watched the black lightning crack across the sky but it didn't disappear like lightning would. The cracks stretched across the blue, splitting it open. The blue afternoon sky then fell in crumbling pieces down onto them. The world around them was collapsing in on itself. The whole of Tynth was crumbling.

Tick and Tock flew around, dodging the falling debris as best as they could. A chunk of sky hit Tick

on the arm and the fairy swerved in the air. Tock grabbed him as they flew over to the cottages.

The syphon stood up from the ground, a deathly stare in his white eyes. He glanced at the fairies. And Cora's heart dropped.

Kaede stretched out his hand and grabbed hold of Tick and Tock with his magic. They kicked and clawed in the air against his magical grasp.

Cora clicked her fingers and appeared in front of Kaede, but he was expecting her. He held his hand out, and it sent her flying across the grass.

Cora wasted no time. She got up, her shoulder aching worse now. She ran at the syphon. Then she clicked her fingers and holding onto the Jinx magic she collided with the syphon like a steam train sending him barrelling in the opposite direction, his hold on Tick and Tock vanishing.

Cora panted. She watched as the syphon stood up once more, and groaned. *Crud.*

'Kaede! We must go!' Archibald cried out. He stumbled over to the syphon.

Unsteadily, Kaede wiped his bloodied nose on the silver sleeve of his robe. Cora could see that one of his arms hung limply by his side, and his right leg was broken. With an angry shout, he held his hand up to the sky.

Cora watched as the dark Tynth sky above them started to rupture and splinter. Parts of the sky fell heavily to the ground. Tynth was crumbling.

Then Kaede pulled something down towards him. Whatever it was, it went soaring straight at Cora, sizzling in the air. It was a black lightning bolt. Cora clicked her fingers, disappearing out of the way of the magic bolt just in time.

With a click, she appeared back where she stood.

There was a sharp sound behind her.

'Oops,' said the silver-haired man.

Turning, Cora almost fell to her knees. Dot had been hit by the bolt of lightning.

Chapter Forty-Nine

ora froze. Time slowed around her as she watched, eye wide, as Dot clutched her stomach.

'Dot!' Cora cried. She clicked her fingers with the witch's magic and appeared behind the old woman. She held her before she could hit the ground.

'Dot, Dot,' she said, placing her down softly.

The old woman's eyes were closed.

Tick and Tock flew to her side.

'She needs help,' said Cora, she pushed the tears from her eye.

Cora looked up at where the warlock and the syphon stood, rage filling her up. But the grass hills were empty. They had gone. The sky above her was crumbling faster now. The ground rumbled dangerously beneath them but Cora didn't care.

Cora stared down at Dot. Her hands shook as she grabbed Dot's hands in hers.

'Can we take her to The Hollow?' asked Cora.

'The council will just follow us there,' said Tick, shaking his head.

Cora saw Dot's chest rise up and down softly. Cora breathed out in relief.

'Belle,' said Tock. 'We can take her to Belle.'

Tick put his ear to Dot's chest.

Cora remembered the hobgoblin who had helped her with her magic.

'She'll know what to do,' said Tick.

Cora nodded.

'Hold on, Dot,' she said. 'You're going to be okay.' Though she wasn't sure if she believed her own words. Why had she asked Dot to come with them? She should have kept her safe.

Scratch walked over to them. He licked Dot's face and curled up next to her on the ground.

The fairies turned to Cora.

'Are you alright?' Tick asked her, he held his arm close to his chest.

Cora nodded. The scratches across her skin were bleeding but she didn't feel them. And her shoulder still ached from when she was thrown down onto it. But she didn't feel that much either.

The sky above them rumbled like thunder. More parts of afternoon blue plummeted down faster like tumbling bricks, crashing to the ground and splitting the grassy fields apart.

'We need to go,' said Tick.

Tock hovered in the air, zapping falling sky parts that fell in their direction into small pieces.

From the ground, Cora looked up and stared out at the crumbling town of Tynth. The cottages. The rolling green hills. The afternoon sky. It was the place where she had once lived. Where her family had once lived. And she had made it back ... just in time to see it disappear.

Cora still had so many questions. Everything she had learnt about herself, about her family ... about the silver-haired man. The man who had attacked her family.

The man who said she had a … *a brother.*

Cora glanced down at Dot.

'Cora,' said Tock. The ground split open near them, opening wide into darkness. 'We have to go.'

The fairies flew down to Cora and held onto Scratch, Dot and her.

Holding tightly to Dot, Cora nodded at the fairies. It was time to go.

And with a *POP!* of magic, Cora, Tick, Tock, Dot and Scratch all disappeared from the crumbling syphon sanctuary that was once her home.

to be continued …

Rebecca McRitchie would love to tell you that she was raised by wolves in the depths of a snow-laden forest until she stumbled upon and saved a village from the fiery peril of a disgruntled dragon.

But, truthfully, she works as a children's book editor and lives in Sydney.

Whimsy and Woe and the sequel, *Whimsy and Woe: The Final Act*, were her first fiction titles, followed by the Jinxed! series.

Sharon O'Connor is a freelance illustrator who lives in Melbourne with her husband and triplet sons.

Since graduating from R.M.I.T. Graphic Design, she has spent many years designing and illustrating in publishing, textiles and packaging with a particular love of character design. In her spare time she likes to paint, bake macarons, hang out with animals and take lots of photos.

The WHIMSY & WOE duology
by Rebecca McRitchie
illustrated by Sonia Kretschmar

After being abandoned by their thespian parents, Whimsy and Woe Mordaunt are left in the care of their austere Aunt Apoline.

Forced to work in Apoline's boarding house, slaving at the beck and call of outlandish and demanding guests, and sharpening the thorns of every plant in the poisonous plant garden, Whimsy and Woe lose all hope that their parents will ever return. Until one day, quite by accident, the siblings stumble upon a half-charred letter that sets them on a course to freedom and finding their parents.

'Adventurous and outlandish, *Whimsy and Woe*
will hook kids in from the first page'
Books+Publishing ★★★★